VALENTINE'S DAY
1946

SEQUEL TO THE
CHRISTMASTIME SERIES

LINDA MAHKOVEC

Design and distribution by Bublish

ISBN: 978-1-647046-72-9 (paperback)
ISBN: 978-1-647046-73-6 (eBook)

Other Books by Linda Mahkovec

The Garden House

And So We Dream

The Notebooks of Honora Gorman:
Fairytales, Whimsy, and Wonder

The Christmastime Series

Christmastime 1939: Prequel to
the Christmastime Series

Christmastime 1940: A Love Story

Christmastime 1941: A Love Story

Christmastime 1942: A Love Story

Christmastime 1943: A Love Story

Christmastime 1944: A Love Story

Christmastime 1945: A Love Story

Short Collections

The Dreams of Youth

Seven Tales of Love

Chapter 1

෨

Lillian sat at her kitchen table with various art supplies spread before her. The low gurgle and hiss of the radiators filled the small apartment with soothing background noise and chased away the chill. She took a sip of tea and studied the two Valentine's Day cards she had painted. They needed something else. After a moment's consideration, she added a few dots of metallic gold paint and smiled at the effect – a hint of elegance now adorned the otherwise homey watercolors.

She leaned back to view the images. For her sister Annette, she had painted a red scalloped heart framed by a wide border that depicted her orchard – the trees hung with red heart-shaped apples. For Charles' sister Kate, a garden reminiscent of the one on her farm, with hearts around the edges.

Both images filled her with longing for the women in her life. How she would love to take a morning walk through the farmyard with Kate, or an evening stroll through the orchard with her sister.

She placed her chin in her hand. And then there was Izzy. Still in England with Red since Christmas. The few letters she had received from her were filled with an underlying happiness, despite some of the grim scenes she described. Though the city was full of rubble and weary soldiers were still returning from distant shores, there was a sense of hope. A belief that better times lay ahead. Any mention of Red positively glowed with love and admiration – the descriptions of him with the patients he cheered on in the hospital, the cozy pubs where he and Izzy often met for dinner, their walks along the little village stream.

And yet. Nothing was mentioned of their plans. Would they return to the States? Would they begin a life together? Or would they go their separate ways?

Her thoughts were interrupted by the sound of hurried footsteps on the stairs – only Gabriel moved with such eagerness. Only Gabriel could make running up the stairs sound like happiness.

She turned to face the door, waiting for the joyful entry he always made.

The door flew open.

"Hi, Mom!" Gabriel quickly dropped his voice when he saw the bassinette with Charlotte sound asleep. He tiptoed over and smiled at her. Then he shrugged off his coat, hung it on the hall tree, and stood at the table looking at the cards.

"Let me guess." He pointed to the garden. "That's for Aunt Kate. And that one's for Aunt Annette."

Lillian smiled and nodded. "I want to send them our family photograph so I thought I might as well combine it with Valentine's Day." She lifted a copy of the recent studio photograph. Charles held Charlotte on his lap, and the boys stood behind her and Charles. Though it had taken several attempts, miraculously it was a good picture of all of them.

"What about a card for Izzy?"

Lillian sighed. "I don't think it would get there in time, with the mail being so slow." The truth was she worried that a Valentine's Day card might strike the wrong tone for Izzy. "I'll send her the photo when I next write to her."

She glanced at the clock. "I thought you were working all day today."

"Yep. Running errands for Mr. G and thought I'd eat something before I head back." He opened the refrigerator and looked inside. "Business is slow, so we're cleaning the merchandise and repairing things."

Lillian got up and squeezed his shoulder. "I'll fix you a sandwich." Gabriel was always hungry. She would have to start packing more food for his lunches.

He quickly finished the peanut butter and jelly sandwich, downed a glass of milk, and grabbed his coat.

"See you at dinner!" And he was off.

She gave a small laugh and watched him run down the stairs, taking two at a time, and then using the banister post to swing around to the next flight – he was almost aerial.

After putting a few final touches on the cards, she set them aside to dry, and rinsed her brushes and palette. She wanted to make a baked chicken meal for Charles. She never thought she would derive so much pleasure from cooking, but Charles relished all her meals, which delighted her to no end. And she could always count on Tommy and Gabriel to eat with gusto. *Tom*, she thought, correcting herself. Tommy wanted to be called "Tom" now.

She checked on Charlotte, kissed her forehead, and put away her art supplies.

Gabriel whistled as he hurried to The Red String Curio Store. He loved Saturdays, his only full day, and was eager to get back. He didn't want to miss out on anything.

He tucked the bag from the hardware store under his arm, and went out of his way to step on the snowy parts of the sidewalk. He liked the crunch of the frozen snow under his feet. When he pushed open the door to the shop, he gave it a little back and forth jiggle to make the silver bell ring even more.

"I'm back!" He set the paper bag on the counter and lifted out the contents. "Spot remover, silver polish, furniture tacks, and glue."

"Excellent. We can really go to town now. Have everything in tip-top shape and sparkling." Mr. G was polishing a set of drinking glasses that he had lined up on the front counter.

"I stopped off at home for a sandwich." Gabriel looked around as he put on the green apron. Except for a few customers who browsed leisurely through the aisles, the shop was empty.

"This set of glasses will complete the top shelf." Mr. G held up a cobalt blue tumbler edged in gold filigree and gave it a final rub with the cloth.

"What's next?"

Mr. G leaned his head to one side as he scanned the shelves. "We might as well be methodical about it. Why don't we work on the teapot collection and that section of the shelves?"

In between assisting customers, they polished the collection of glasses, teapots, teacups, and serving trays, cleaned the shelves, and rearranged the items. Then they began on the next section, full of Toby jugs and mugs, beer steins, and heavy earthenware drinking vessels.

They chuckled and made comments as they dusted the character mugs – stout publicans, weathered sailors, mustached men in top hats and bow ties, others in tri-corner hats or scrolled white wigs, cobblers, grocers, jailors with keys, clowns and court jesters – winking, leering, grinning – most of them in fair condition.

"What's the difference between Toby jugs and Toby mugs?" Gabriel asked.

"The jugs are for pouring – see how this tricorn forms a spout? The mugs are for drinking." Mr. G lifted a squinty-eyed pirate. "There's a rascal, if I ever saw one!"

Gabriel polished a jovial innkeeper. "This man looks like he'd be fun. Hey, here's a lady. I think."

Mr. G held up the stern-faced matron. "Rather formidable, isn't she? Most of the collection feature men. I've clumped the few female mugs together here."

"Like her," Gabriel said, lifting another mug to polish. "She seems happy."

Mr. G nodded at the old crone. "As well she should be. Sairy Gamp, in her cups. Dickens, you know."

"Her cups?" Gabriel asked.

"Three sheets to the wind, as they say."

"Sheets?"

"She's a tippler." Seeing that Gabriel was still confused, Mr. G mimed drinking and then staggered a bit. "Inebriated."

"Oh! She drinks too much."

Mr. G inspected another mug. "This Queen of Hearts is more recent."

"We could put her out for Valentine's Day. It's coming up."

"Perhaps," Mr. G said with a dubious air. "I believe this is the moment she cries, 'Off with their heads!'"

"Not very romantic, is she?" Gabriel held up a sea captain with a mermaid. "Maybe this one would be better."

By the end of day, three sections of shelves had been dusted and the merchandise polished. Mr. G let out a deep sigh as the last customer departed, having purchased a single Victorian hat pin. While Gabriel took the broom and swept around the counter, Mr. G flipped through his ledger.

"Sales were good for the holidays. Excellent, in fact. It was one of the best years for the shop, what with the war over and everyone happy. Ready to pick up where they left off." He glanced out at the empty shop. "This time of year is always a bit of a letdown. The bustle of Thanksgiving and Christmas is just a memory, the hope of the New Year has come and gone. Winter has set in." He released another sigh and took off his apron. "Ah well. Must get through the doldrums as best we can."

Gabriel wasn't used to seeing Mr. G down-hearted. "What would help? More sales?"

Mr. G gave a loud chuckle. "It most certainly would, Gabriel. That's exactly what I'm talking about. Well, sales, and more – life! The business of helping people find the right items, chatting with them, hearing their news…"

"Maybe I can help. As your number one employee." Gabriel put the broom away and stood in front of the calendar on the wall. He lifted his right hand, as if weighing ideas. "Well, here we are, almost in February. Could be a long winter. That might keep people home." He raised his other palm. "On the other hand, they might enjoy being here, doing a bit of browsing. Or," raising his right hand again, "people might be busy with their families. On the other hand, they might be looking for company, like Dusty and Junior."

"How many hands do you have, Gabriel?" Mr. G tucked the ledger back under the counter. The grandfather clock in the back chimed six stately bongs. "Time to wrap up."

Gabriel turned the calendar to February and placed his finger on the 14th. "Look here! Valentine's Day. Do you do anything special for that?"

"Oh, I display the Victorian cards. I usually sell a few pieces of jewelry and the like."

Gabriel hung his shop apron next to Mr. G's. "How about we do something different this year? We could have a Valentine's Day – event. Kind of like the party we had when Tommy and Amy made the apple tart for their French class."

Mr. G smiled at the memory. "We rather enjoyed ourselves that day, didn't we? However, that was a gathering of friends. What do you have in mind for Valentine's Day?"

"I don't know yet, but I'll come up with something. Mind if I borrow my thinking cap?" He reached for an old bowler he sometimes wore at the shop. "It might help." He slipped on his coat and put the hat on his head with a tap.

"By all means." He chuckled at the enthusiasm Gabriel could pull out of the air at will. "I'll see you next week."

"So long, Mr. G!" The happiness of the little bell seemed to linger in the shop, even after Gabriel left.

Chapter 2

∽

Kate's breakfast table was crowded and lively, even with Eugene and his wife still away at her family's house in Iowa. Jimmy and his wife, Gladys, sat side by side, and Paul sat across from them. Frankie was in his high chair with Ursula next to him, feeding him oatmeal. And Kate and Jessica were still bringing plates of food to the table – eggs, fried potatoes, sausages, and toast.

Though the farmyard outside was white with snow, inside was warm and full of the robust scents of coffee and a farmhouse breakfast.

Jimmy and Jessica had been verbally sparring and neither was prepared to give up any ground.

"I'm just saying that nobody likes to be set up," said Jimmy.

"Especially those two," added Paul, with an exaggerated shiver, and speared another sausage.

"I'm not *setting them up*. I just think they might enjoy each other's company. A bit. Maybe. From time to time." Jessica looked to Kate for help. "Mom?"

Kate gave it some thought, and then shook her head. "Try as I might, I can't see it, either. I'm afraid you're outnumbered on this one. And that's without Eugene here," she added with a laugh. "We all know how he'd vote."

Jessica put a fist on her hip and looked out at the happy eaters. "Where's your imagination?" She turned to her sister. "Ursula?"

Ursula used the spoon to wipe oatmeal from Frankie's chin. He banged his hands on the tray top, laughed when he got everyone's attention, and banged on it again.

"It's a lovely thought, Jessica. And of course, it would be nice. But —" She thought of the incident that had happened just after Christmas. She had never told anyone about it. "I think Mr. Creight is still too raw from the pain of losing Jeremy. I wouldn't want to burden him with anything right now."

"Burden!" Jessica sat down and gave an emphatic scoot of her chair forward. "Companionship is not a burden." She reached for a piece of toast and began buttering it.

"Unless it's forced on you," said Jimmy.

Jessica was about to defend herself again but changed her mind. "Clem will help me. At least with Mrs. Fletcher."

Jimmy winced as if in pain. "Just the idea of those two."

Gladys had slipped into the role of peacemaker in the family. Though only married to Jimmy for a few weeks, she had a subtle way of shifting quarrelsome conversations to more agreeable subjects.

She looked slyly at Paul. "I ran into Ingrid Fogel. She said you were going to take her to the cinema over in Greenfield."

"That's right. And tomorrow I'm going over to Becky's for dinner. Saturday, Peg and I are going to an ice-skating party."

"Clem and I are going too," said Jessica. "We're taking Donny with us."

Ursula watched Paul as he spoke. "What about Lucille? You haven't spent much time with her since you've been back." Lucille was the only girl Paul had ever shown any real interest in. At least before he left for the Pacific.

"She looked so beautiful at the wedding, didn't she?" said Jessica. "In that pale blue silk two-piece. She always dresses with such style. You should call her, Paul. Ask her to the Valentine's Day dance."

He shrugged as if it didn't matter. "If she wants. Though she always has her nose in a book."

"Well, she does work at the library," said Gladys.

"She's so good with the children," said Jessica. "I love watching her read to the little ones. Besides," she asked, turning to Paul, "how would you know what she does? You've only called on her once since you've been back."

"And I saw her at the wedding. That's twice."

Jessica shook her head at Paul. "One of the prettiest girls in town and you act like you're indifferent. I'm not convinced."

Paul held up a hand. "None of your match-making for me, Jess."

"Leave him alone," said Jimmy. "He's playing the field. A good strategy."

His comment earned him an arched eyebrow from Gladys. "Well, don't play too long or all your choices will be taken."

"Gladys is right," Kate said with a smile. "At any rate, Paul, you'll have to make a decision soon about the dance. It's only a few weeks away. And with more and more boys returning every day, you could be left without a partner."

"I'll take that chance," Paul added with a grin.

"That reminds me," said Jessica. "We're meeting with Sue Ellen and Shirley today to talk about decorations for the dance. Want to come, Gladys? We could use your help. And Sue Ellen is trying out a new recipe for lunch."

Gladys gave a laugh. "I'd love to."

The rest of the breakfast followed in amicable conversation. Kate mentioned that Ed would be over later in the morning to go over the list of machinery repairs. She turned to Gladys. "Now that my sons have returned, Ed doesn't come as often. I think he and Opal are enjoying the extra time together."

"I think you're right," said Gladys. "They come into Arnold's now and then to do some shopping and then have lunch at the café."

"And they're always holding hands, which just goes to show you." Jessica stated this as if it supported her matchmaking idea. "You're never too old for love. Or companionship."

After the table was cleared and the dishes were washed, Jimmy and Paul went out with Kate to walk the farmyard and check on the animals. Jessica and Gladys sat at the table and enjoyed another cup of coffee together, discussing the Valentine's Day dance.

Ursula bundled up Frankie in his red hooded coat and matching mittens and pulled him along on the little sled that Jimmy and Paul had fashioned for him. It had a little seat to prevent him from tumbling over the sides. He loved nothing more than to be pulled through the snow.

The outdoor temperature felt invigorating after the warmth of the kitchen, and Ursula took in several deep breaths of the clean, sharp air. Her thoughts wandered to Mr. Creight and her gratitude to him. She replayed the goodbye she was able to say to Friedrich, thanks to Creight. She would never forget it.

That was over a month ago, already. Ursula was grateful for every day that Friedrich remained at Camp Shanks in New York, on U.S. soil. It meant that he was still safe. She dreaded the day he would have to ship out to a work camp somewhere in Europe. At least now they could write to one another, and he still felt a part of her life. Once he left, she feared their communication would lessen. Or disappear altogether.

As Ursula pulled Frankie on the sled, her thoughts went to the day not long after Christmas when she had come upon Mr. Creight. She had walked farther than she usually did with Frankie.

Her mind had been full of Friedrich and his sudden departure. She had pulled Frankie across the snow-covered fields, and then crossed the frozen stream that bordered land owned by Abe Creight.

She had stopped to point out two deer foraging around the creek – much to Frankie's delight – and then pulled the sled up the low slope of the bank.

Through the bare trees and brambles, she had seen Mr. Creight leaning against the fencing in his field. She wondered what he was doing, standing so still, apparently deep in thought. Then she stiffened in fear as it flashed upon her – the way he held the shotgun angled towards him.

She had screamed his name and ran to him.

Creight's face was wet with tears and his eyes sharpened in anger at her intrusion. They stood frozen for several moments. Then Creight put a hand over his eyes and his shoulders slumped. When he looked up, a shadow of shame filled his eyes. He met her eyes, once, and then turned away. He fixed his gaze on the horizon.

Ursula kept her eyes on him, unable to control the trembling in her body. Neither spoke. Then Frankie, wanting to be pulled, broke the silence with his cries.

Creight gave an almost imperceptible tip of his head. "Your boy needs you. Go."

Ursula had run back and gathered Frankie in her arms, and returned to Creight. He had broken open the gun and was pocketing the shells.

Ursula took a step towards him. "Mr. Creight."

But Creight had simply taken his gun and walked away. Her eyes followed him as he traipsed through the frozen field, corn stubble poking up through the snow. His figure grew smaller and smaller against the expanse of white, utterly alone under the leaden gray sky. Ursula had dropped to the ground, holding Frankie tightly and rocking him as she wept. For Creight, for herself, for the overwhelming pain in the world.

In the days that followed, Ursula filled with all the things she wanted to say to Mr. Creight. To let him know how important he was to her. That she didn't have a father, and Frankie didn't have a grandfather. That they needed him. That he would break her heart if he... But those were words that could not be spoken to a man like Creight. She knew better than to try.

Instead, she had driven past his farm from time to time to see if he was active, and felt a tremendous relief if she saw him carrying wood, or moving between the house and outbuildings, or even if the lights were on.

A few times she had stopped by with baked goods for him and exchanged a few words. Each trip she had brought Frankie with her. Besides adding happiness to the encounters, Frankie's babbling and toddling kept the conversation light and brief. On her last visit, Creight had called out to her as she was leaving.

"Ursula!" He took a few steps towards her but kept his eyes on the bare trees by the road. "No need to worry about me. I'm a practical man. That –"

He gestured to the field with his head. "It's behind me now."

She hadn't seen him again until a week before the double wedding for Eugene and Edna, and Jimmy and Gladys. She and Eugene had driven over to Creight's farm and handed him an invitation, saying how much it would mean to them if he would attend.

They didn't believe he would come and were surprised to see him at the reception. Ursula understood that it was his way of letting her know he was all right and not to worry about him. He even seemed to be making an effort to enjoy himself, especially when she put Frankie on his lap.

Everything at that moment had seemed fine, happy even. But then it all fell apart. Jessica and Clem had been talking with Mrs. Fletcher and brought her over and seated her next to Mr. Creight. With the worst words she could have chosen, Jessica said, "Thought you two could enjoy each other's company. Maybe take a spin or two around the dance floor."

Clem had grown extremely uncomfortable, Creight scowled in outrage, and Mrs. Fletcher snapped her head up at Clem, and then away, as if she had been tricked. Neither Creight nor Mrs. Fletcher had stayed long after that.

Ursula now shook her head at the memories, and pulled Frankie back home on the little sled. She groaned to think that Jessica was still talking about bringing Mr. Creight and Mrs. Fletcher together. Her heart was in the right place but she had picked the exact wrong two people for her matchmaking. Two wounded, proud, prickly loners who resented interference of any kind.

She would have to try to dissuade Jessica.

Frankie's babbling brought her back to the present moment. "You want to go faster?" Ursula began to lightly run, her heart filling with happiness at Frankie's howls of laughter.

Chapter 3

Lillian loved this time of day. Her work on the book illustrations finished for the day, dinner in the oven and already filling the apartment with a cozy aroma, the boys and Charles on their way home, and Charlotte – fresh from her nap and fed – full of energy and eager to play.

She sat on the couch holding Charlotte. All the little hallmarks of babyhood for Tommy and Gabriel were coming back to her. At four months old, Charlotte enjoyed this upright position, bouncing tentatively on her chubby legs.

"What a big girl you are!" Lillian laughed when Charlotte's bouncing ended in a delighted collapse. Lillian lifted her high and kissed her tiny feet.

She kept a close eye on the clock as she awaited the arrival of Tommy and Gabriel from their volunteer evening at the hospital. They were with Henry, so she wasn't worried. Still, she never fully relaxed until everyone was home again – like a mother hen with her wings spread around her brood.

She heard voices on the stairs and running feet. In a sing-song voice she said to Charlotte, "I think someone's home!"

"Hi, Mom!" Tommy and Gabriel tossed their coats onto the hall tree and went to the couch. "Hello, Charlotte!"

Charlotte's face broke into a smile and her tiny fists went to her mouth.

Tommy and Gabriel sat on either side of Lillian and soon had Charlotte giggling.

Gabriel waved a letter that he had already ripped open. "I got a letter from Tiny! And you –" he said, handing an envelope to Lillian, "got one from Izzy."

Lillian's face lit up, and Tommy reached over to hold Charlotte. He nuzzled his forehead against hers while Lillian read her letter.

Gabriel tucked his letter back in the envelope. "Tiny says hello to you all. And you too!" he said to Charlotte. He picked up his old teddy bear, Taffy, and walked the bear over to her and tickled her tummy, making her laugh.

Tommy looked up at Lillian as she folded the letter. "How's Izzy?"

"Fine. Keeping busy. She's helping out with a children's organization there." Lillian was soon laughing along with Tommy and Gabriel at Charlotte's earnest bubble blowing.

"I'm glad she's finally getting older," Gabriel said. "She's more to fun to play with now that she's not sleeping all the time." He made the bear jump up and down next to Charlotte.

"She tried to roll over today," said Lillian. "The way she's growing, I'm going to have to get a playpen soon." She looked out at the small living room in dismay. "Though I don't know where I'll put it. There's not a spare inch here." She glanced at the short half-wall that separated the kitchen from the living room. Perhaps she could move the table against the wall during the day and put a playpen in the kitchen?

When Tommy shifted Charlotte to face Gabriel, he noticed Lillian's old-fashioned Valentine's Day cards lining the mantel and a garland of red paper hearts below them. More were strung around the door frames and bookshelves.

"Getting ready for Valentine's Day already?" he asked.

"It's just a few weeks away." She looked out at the decorations. "I've been so absorbed with the illustrations for the boys' adventure story that I thought it would be a nice change. Give the dragons and evil warlocks a break. How was the hospital? Did Henry ride back with you?"

"He always does, Mom," said Gabriel. "He said Mrs. Kuntzman was making schnitzel and spaetzle tonight. You know how he loves that."

Tommy bounced Charlotte lightly on his lap and looked over at the clock. "Where's Dad?"

"He called to say he might be a little late."

Gabriel got up and inspected the heart garlands. "Maybe we should do this for Valentine's Day at the Red String. They look cheerful. Might help with sales."

"Still thinking of ways to drum up business?" Lillian asked, getting started on dinner. She opened the oven door, took a quick look at the bubbling dish, and turned off the oven.

Gabriel nodded. "We talked about a few ideas. Mr. G says we could display Valentine's Day cards and merchandise and put up some decorations. But we need something else. My turn." He raised his arms out to Charlotte and lifted her. He carried her around the living room, pointing out the hearts and the images on the cards.

"What are we having?" asked Tommy, joining Lillian in the kitchen. "It smells good."

"Just meatloaf and a salad. And Mrs. Kuntzman made a pie for you boys – chocolate cream. I stopped by to say hello on my way to the post office and she told me to come back in an hour. That she had a surprise for you two."

"My favorite!" said Gabriel, coming into the kitchen. "Did you hear that, Charlotte? Wait until you get big enough to eat pie. You're going to love it." He sat at the table and played pat-a-cake with her.

As Lillian prepared the salad, she asked Tommy and Gabriel about the hospital. She still volunteered one night a week and knew many of the patients who were well enough to participate in the recreation room activities. "Anything new?"

Tommy's mouth twitched in concern. "Kind of. We were helping to set up a new jigsaw puzzle and two guys started to fight. First they were just arguing, then they started hitting each other. Henry helped to break them apart."

Lillian turned around and waited to hear more. There were often arguments and good-natured teasing but rarely fist fights.

"One of them was Matty Cavendish – you know, they guy who –" Tommy gestured to his leg. "He had just yelled at his fiancée and told her not to come back. He said it was over."

"Matty. I know who you mean. He sat in on my drawing class but didn't participate. I didn't know he had a fiancée. Who was he fighting with?"

"His friend Mel. Mel told him he was a dope for chasing her away." Tommy shook his head. "Matty fights with a lot of people. He's always mad or unhappy. The only person he's different around is Gabriel."

"What do you mean?" Lillian brought plates to the table and placed them at each seat.

Tommy began to set the silverware around the table. "It's hard to explain."

"Give me an example," Lillian said, curious to know more.

"Well, like a couple of weeks ago. Matty was arguing with everybody, refusing to have any visitors, yelling at the nurses who wanted him to use the artificial leg. It was Gabriel who got him to try it. No one else could convince him. Gabriel sat next to him and said: 'must be hard to walk with just one leg.'

"Everyone turned away, expecting an explosion. Then Matty started to laugh. Gabriel held up the leg and said, 'This looks pretty interesting. Can I see how it works?'"

When Lillian looked over at Gabriel, he gave a shrug. "I was curious."

"Next thing, there was Matty trying out his new leg. He can walk pretty good now, but he's still angry all the time."

Lillian went to the salad bowl on the counter and ground a little salt and pepper over it. "Internal wounds can be harder to diagnose. And treat." She added vinegar and oil to the salad and tossed it. "Sometimes I think two nights a week at the hospital is too much for you, Tommy. Tom. With school and your work at Mancetti's."

"It's not too much, Mom. I like going. Besides, it won't last forever." Tommy picked up a carrot stick and bit into it.

Lillian was able to keep an eye on the boys the one night she taught class there. She had agreed to let Tommy go an extra night with Henry, and once in a while Gabriel joined them. But she sometimes questioned her decision.

Her worry vanished when she heard the door open. "Charles, you're home!"

He greeted the boys as he slipped out of his coat and hat and hung them on the hall tree. "Sorry I'm late." He went to the table and lifted Charlotte. "There's my girl!" He held her high and laughed at her gurgling.

"That's three times in one week." Lillian lifted her cheek to be kissed as he draped his arm around her.

"Business is booming. Thank goodness. There's so much to do." He glanced at the letters on the counter. "Any news?"

"I got a letter from Tiny," said Gabriel. "He and Molly want to buy a house close to her family. He loves that she has so many brothers and sisters and grandparents and aunts and uncles and cousins. There must be a hundred."

"Tiny!" Charles said, remembering his recent visit. "I still can't believe how much he changed. In my mind, whenever I thought of him, it was as I saw him that evening by the lake in the park. What a transformation."

"And Mom got a letter from Izzy," said Tommy.

Charles knew that would make Lillian happy. "What did she have to say about Rockwell's offer? Or should I say his ultimatum?"

"Back by March or she's sacked?" Lillian shook her head. "Our letters must have crossed, so there was no mention of that. Even though she should have received it by now."

"Any – update?"

Lillian smiled at Charles's choice of words. "No. She sees Red every day, but there was no mention of their plans. I can see them there – strolling through the village, having dinner together." In a softer voice she said to Charles, "She reminded me that it was five years ago that they were engaged, and how happy they had been. And then –" she popped open her hands – "everything changed."

"The war," said Tommy.

"*And* he married his nurse," Gabriel added.

Lillian lifted the meatloaf out of the oven, wondering when she would learn. Anytime she lowered her voice to Charles, the boys automatically paid closer attention.

Charles silently rocked Charlotte in his arms. "I'm grateful Izzy is there, whatever they decide."

"Let's eat!" said Lillian, setting the hot dish on a trivet in the middle of the table. "I'm hungry."

Charles placed Charlotte in her bassinette and they all sat around the table. They were soon enjoying the simple meal.

Charles gestured to the living room as he took a helping of meatloaf. "I see the mood has shifted to Valentine's Day. Any more thoughts for the Red String, Gabriel?"

"Mr. G and I were talking about it yesterday. I want it to be really special. Different from other years."

"I'll help," said Tommy. "And Amy and Mickey will want to."

"Thanks. The more the many-er."

"You mean the merrier?" asked Lillian.

"That, too," Gabriel said. "Henry always says 'the more the many-er!'"

Tommy laughed. "I'll bet he'll want to be a part of it."

"And I'll get Billy to help," said Gabriel. "He's good at thinking up stuff."

Lillian and Charles exchanged a smile at the understatement.

Tommy turned to Lillian. "What about those parties you had at Rockwell Publishing. How did you make those special?"

"Let me think. We had some really good ones. Especially with Izzy in charge," she added with a laugh. "There were always plenty of refreshments. A table set up with a spread of food. And drinks. That was always the focal point, where everyone would gather. And music, of course. And we often had a raffle at the end. War bonds, usually."

She glanced over at Charles and noted the same maddening private smile she had noticed lately. There was a mysterious air about him, as if he was secretly pleased about something.

Gabriel had been turning the raffle idea over in his mind. "That's it!" he cried, slamming his palm on the table and causing Lillian to jump. "That can be our grand finale. Thanks, Mom! I'll run it by Mr. G tomorrow."

"I'm glad we've solved one issue. Your turn, Charles."

He looked up with a guilty face. "What do you mean?"

"All these late evenings. The mystery when I called your office once or twice."

His face fell. "Did Mrs. Sullivan tell you?"

"Aha, so there is something. Today she said 'you were out again, looking at –' and then caught herself. She was in the middle of training a new clerk and almost gave you away. And the same thing happened last week when one of the accountants answered. I must say you have a loyal staff."

Charles had to smile at the thought of his staff covering for him.

Lillian set her fork down. "Are you expanding the business?"

"No."

"Planning a family trip? With the trains and roads so busy with returning servicemen –"

Gabriel looked up. "Are we going somewhere?"

"No," Charles said, laughing. "Not that either."

"What is it, Dad?" asked Tommy. "You have a secret?"

Charles looked at Lillian, and then the boys. "I was going to save it as a Valentine's Day surprise."

Lillian's eyes brightened. "Now you *have* to tell me. You know I can't stand not knowing."

Charles opened his mouth, and then decided against it.

"Valentine's Day," mused Gabriel, rubbing his chin.

"You're giving Mom some jewelry," Tommy guessed.

Charles shook his head.

"Clothes?" asked Gabriel. "A new dress? Some shoes?"

"Shoes!" Lillian said.

"Give us a hint," said Tommy.

Charles was enjoying the suspense. "It's something you've been wanting for a long time."

Lillian turned her head to the side, trying to remember what she had mentioned. "I can't think of anything I asked for."

"Art supplies?" asked Gabriel.

"No." Charles paused, holding his fork mid-air, and looked up. "Though I suppose there's a connection."

"An easel?" asked Gabriel.

"I don't have room for an easel. And I have all the supplies I need."

"Tickets to an art show? Or a play or something?" Tommy said.

Charles shook his head and took another helping of meatloaf. "Actually, it's something for all of us."

Lillian and the boys looked to one another in confusion.

"All of us?" asked Tommy, perplexed.

Gabriel's eyes widened in excitement. "Another baby!"

"Gabriel!" Lillian cried. She saw that Charles was quietly laughing.

Tommy scoffed. "You think Mom wouldn't know about that?"

Gabriel looked around. "A new radio? A new couch? A trip to Aunt Annette's?"

"Dad already said it wasn't a trip," said Tommy.

"A playpen!" cried Gabriel.

Tommy jerked his head back. "How is that for all of us? We give up, Dad."

"Tell us!" said Lillian. "I can't stand it any longer! Please!"

"Okay, okay," Charles said laughing. He set his utensils down and filled his eyes with Lillian.

"A home. A house. I've been looking at houses. That's why I've been late these past few weeks."

"A house!" Lillian jumped up from her chair, ran to Charles, and flung her arms around him. "Oh, Charles! Did you hear that, boys?"

Tommy and Gabriel bombarded him with questions.

"Where?"

"When?"

"Do I get my own room?"

"So, I can get a bike?"

All the commotion caused Charlotte to cry out, as if she was missing out on the fun and excitement.

Lillian went to lift her. "Charlotte! We're going to have a house! You'll have a yard to play in!" But Charlotte was hungry. While Lillian heated up a bottle, Charles walked with Charlotte until she quieted down, and answered all the questions as best he could.

"You can have a bigger kitchen. And a studio to paint in. Your very own, just like you've always wanted. You need it with the five-book deal you're working on."

"My own studio! I can't believe it!" said Lillian. "I can spread out all my supplies and illustrations."

"And I can really have my own room?" asked Tommy. "Wait until I tell Amy!"

"Wait until I tell Billy! Can I have a treehouse?" Gabriel asked.

As they finished dinner, Charles said yes to everything. Treehouses, a car and garage, a flower garden and a vegetable garden, a washing machine and clothesline, a grass yard, a sandbox, bicycles, a dog and doghouse, birdhouses in all the trees.

"Now!" said Lillian. "How about we celebrate with Mrs. Kuntzman's chocolate pie?"

As soon as the words left her mouth, she felt the tiniest deflation of her euphoria as she realized that moving would mean not living close to her beloved neighbor anymore.

Chapter 4

༄

Jessica brushed her hair in front of the mirror. It was Saturday and she was going into town with Jimmy and Paul and would later drive back with Clem, who was joining them for dinner. She also wanted to look at the dresses at Arnold's. She had tried to convince Ursula to come with them, but as usual, she refused. Ursula didn't say much about Friedrich, but everyone knew that was all she thought about, especially since she hadn't received a letter from him in almost two weeks.

Maybe Ursula would help her with Mr. Creight. Jessica knew that Ursula worried about the older man and now and then brought him food. When Eugene and Jimmy asked why she bothered with the curmudgeon, Ursula said that he was alone now and she thought it helped him to be around Frankie.

Yes, Ursula was the best chance for softening Mr. Creight. She herself would work on Mrs. Fletcher. Jessica placed a barrette on one side of her hair, changed her mind, and took it out. She opened the dresser drawer and pulled out a blue satin ribbon.

She wasn't by nature intrusive – or a matchmaker – she told her reflection, defensively. She respected people's privacy. And believed that most people knew what was best for them. Normally. But then people didn't always behave normally. And sometimes they needed a little nudge, a little encouragement. For the sake of happiness. What could be wrong with that?

Her previous impression of Mrs. Fletcher as a crotchety killjoy had changed lately. She had visited the older woman with Clem and was surprised to find a warmer version, no doubt due to the presence of Clem. And since Clem was close to Mrs. Fletcher, Jessica made it a point to be on good terms with her.

Just after the New Year, Jessica had paid a visit to Mrs. Fletcher on her own, using a freshly baked applesauce cake as an excuse to stop by. She had expected a scowl and a curt nod, but Mrs. Fletcher smiled when she opened the door for Jessica.

"Why, thank you, Jessica. Come inside and enjoy a cup of coffee with me and we'll sample this. Looks delicious."

"I hope so. I sweetened it with corn syrup and molasses. It's frustrating, isn't it? The war's over, but sugar is still rationed."

"Guess it's fitting – sugar was the first food to be rationed and it'll be the last. I've grown used to taking my coffee unsweetened. I don't think I could drink it any other way now. Have a seat while I boil the water."

They sat at the small kitchen table and sipped on coffee and enjoyed the cake.

Mrs. Fletcher gave a nod of approval. "It's just right."

The conversation flowed with ease and Jessica was soon describing the challenges and delights of her job as a student teacher, and her upcoming wedding with Clem in the spring. They discussed the books they were reading, and Mrs. Fletcher talked about her love of music. And they talked about the recent snowfall and the colder temperatures.

"Once the milder weather arrives, we can have our coffee at the table outside. The garden's so lovely in the spring."

Jessica had the impression that the older woman was different, almost cheerful. "You seem happy today, Mrs. Fletcher. I mean –"

"Not my usual grouchy self?"

"No! No. I mean… I don't know what I mean." Jessica gave a light laugh and took a sip of coffee.

"I think you're right. Before you came, I was listening to some music and looking out at my garden – thinking that life goes on and we must make the best of it. Don't you think?"

Jessica set her cup down. "I do. I do think that."

Mrs. Fletcher tilted her head at Jessica, as if weighing something. She rose to her feet. "I'd like to play you something. The record Clem brought me, the piano music by Liszt. Would you like to hear it?"

"I would! I know Clem picked it out especially for you." Jessica felt privileged that something personal was being shared with her. "Called Solace, or Peace or something."

"*Consolation*," Mrs. Fletcher called from the living room.

Jessica cut two more slices of cake for them while Mrs. Fletcher placed the disc on the record player, and turned it on.

Jessica heard a few scratchy sounds from the needle. Then, delicate, hauntingly beautiful piano music filled the air. She stopped chewing and listened.

Mrs. Fletcher came back into the kitchen and quietly sipped her coffee. She smiled at Jessica's upturned face. There was something pure and lovely in the way the girl opened herself to the music, connecting with it. Mrs. Fletcher felt a rush of affection for Jessica and knew that Clem had chosen right. As he had with the music.

The music wove its way from unease and ache into peaceful resolution, echoing the opening wistfulness, but resolving into hope. The piece ended, and the needle came to the end of the record.

"Ohhh," Jessica said softly, her eyes peering at some internal vision of beauty. "It tells a story, doesn't it? All those high and low notes intertwined. That there is sadness and sorrow – yet mixed with all the pain, there is also beauty and peace and such gentleness. And that everything will be – *is* – all right." She lifted her face to Mrs. Fletcher. "Is that what you hear?"

Mrs. Fletcher softly nodded. "Clem was right. It always improves my mood. I'm sometimes inclined to dark thoughts. Especially since losing Martin. Gardening and being outside helps – but in the winter I'm stuck inside, and I'm apt to brood. So, I listen to my collection of music and find that it helps. And this piece – well, you can hear for yourself."

"It's beautiful. Can you play it again?"

After listening to it a second time, Jessica nodded, as if more fully understanding it.

Mrs. Fletcher patted Jessica's arm, and went to turn the record player off. She returned to the kitchen and refilled their cups.

"You know, the first time I listened to it, I fought what I was feeling. I knew it was beautiful, but I set it aside. I let a few weeks go by. Then I listened to it again. And I let myself feel, really feel the music. I turned it up and let myself be surrounded by it.

"And then I played it again. And again. That tenderness – it cut through my grief and reached beyond my pain, and I felt my boy again. The love and joy." She pressed her hand to her heart. "And I knew that I would always feel Martin here with me. He's a part of me, and that will never change.

"It was like I saw things from afar. I understood that the world is full of beauty, that it's always there, though sometimes hidden. I went to the back door and looked out at the sunset. It was achingly lovely. You know – pinks, streaks of purple, gold – and I felt, for the first time since Martin's death, that there was still hope."

She turned to Jessica and gave a little laugh. "For what, I don't even know. But my heart opened. That's it – my heart opened. And I *wanted* to feel the world again. I wanted to let it in."

Jessica gave a soft smile, understanding what she was describing.

"Then I walked out into my wintery, crumpled garden. I walked to where the irises would bloom, and I stood in front of the trellis where my roses would climb, and ran my hand along the cold wisteria vines – and it was as if I could see them in bloom. I swear I caught of waft of springtime sweetness. It was like the whole garden was alive, with bees buzzing and butterflies flitting about and birds warbling. I stood out there until the sun went down." She laughed again. "Then I realized how cold I was and came inside and made a cup of tea."

They sat in silence for a few moments, lingering in the effect of the music, and in their own thoughts. Then they remembered their coffee and cake in front of them.

Mrs. Fletcher was about to take another sip but paused in thought, using both hands to hold the cup. "Beauty is a strange thing, isn't it? Something so small – a melody, a sunset, a winter garden – can open into worlds of loveliness and transform us. Even if just for a moment." She turned to Jessica. "Clem did that. That boy brought me peace and he's been so utterly kind to me. Kindness is another form of beauty, don't you think? I'm glad you two have each other. That makes me happy."

Jessica smiled at her words. "I'm glad, too. I'm glad we'll be living in town and I can come and see your garden in the spring."

Since that day in early January and her new-found appreciation of Mrs. Fletcher, Jessica felt that it was wrong for someone who could feel so much to be all alone.

And though she fought against it, the image of Mr. Creight kept creeping into her mind. She frowned at the memory of the wedding, and her not so subtle matchmaking. She had been too heavy handed, caught up in all the happiness of the wedding, and the apparent ease of love.

Jessica adjusted the blue ribbon in her hair. She told herself that first tries were always a little uneven. But at least the idea had been put out there. At least she had forced the possibility into the minds of both Mrs. Fletcher and Mr. Creight.

"I consider that progress," she said, with a nod to her reflection.

"Jess! Hurry up! We're ready to leave," Jimmy hollered from downstairs.

"Coming!"

*

Luck was with her. She knew that Abe Creight often went into town on Saturday and she now smiled to see him tossing a bag of feed into the bed of his pickup truck. Dressed, as usual, in his tan-colored canvas overalls and matching chore coat. Always working.

"There's Mr. Creight. I'm going to see if he can help Mrs. Fletcher with her garden gate."

"In the snow?" asked Paul.

"I mean her back door."

"Clem and I can do that," said Jimmy, pulling into a parking space on the town square.

"I'll help," said Paul.

"No," said Jessica. "I want it to be Mr. Creight."

Her scheming dawned on them and Jimmy groaned. "Don't you go stirring up trouble."

"Really, Jess. I don't know of two colder, hard-nosed loners," said Paul.

"Mrs. Fletcher – and Abe Creight?" Jimmy gave a hearty laugh. "You've got some imagination. The only sparks that would fly with those two would be flint against flint!"

"We'll see," said Jessica. "Oh, look – there's Lucille."

"Where? Where?" Paul bolted up in his seat and his head snapped around, searching for Lucille.

"Just as I thought," Jessica said with a grin. "Huh – I must have been mistaken."

Jimmy took off his cap and swatted Paul on the head. "Looks like you're a goner, for all that playing the field business."

Paul colored at being so easily found out and impatiently pushed open the truck door.

"Go on, Cupid," Jimmy said to Jessica. "We'll see you later at home."

Jessica crossed the street and went up to Mr. Creight.

"Hello, Mr. Creight. How're you faring?"

Creight nodded his reply as he slammed the tailgate shut. "You?"

"I'm just off to see Clem. He's coming to dinner tonight."

"How's Ursula?"

"She's fine. Funny you should ask. Ursula was just talking about you, saying how handy you are with mending things." She placed her hand on his arm, as if just striking upon an idea. "Do you have a minute? Could you give Clem some advice on a few repairs? There's a back gate that doesn't swing right or something."

Creight cast his eyes about, searching for an excuse. He didn't want to get involved. He wasn't a carpenter or a builder.

"Five minutes. That's all it should take. We can walk there. It's just up the street."

"All right, then. Can't promise anything. I do repairs around the house and farm. That's about it."

Jessica talked unceasingly as she led him the few blocks to Mrs. Fletcher's house. "Here we are."

Abe stopped when he saw where they were. "Thought you said —"

"Clem helps Mrs. Fletcher now and then. Visits her. Now that she's all alone. Clem and Martin were friends, you know."

Doubt filled Creight's face and stayed there, as he remembered the wedding.

Jessica ran up the steps and knocked on Mrs. Fletcher's door.

The porch door soon opened to the older woman drying her hands on a dish towel. "Hello,

Jessica! How nice —" Her hands stopped moving and her smile dropped. Her eyes shot from Jessica to Mr. Creight and back.

"I was just telling Mr. Creight about that squeaky door and how it doesn't close right. I thought he could take a look. Help Clem with it." Jessica smiled. "May we?"

Mrs. Fletcher held the door open for them. She was suspicious of Jessica's intentions but didn't want to jump to conclusions. Clem *had* been helping her with a few things around the house. Well, a dripping faucet. She certainly didn't need Abe Creight or anyone else to —

Jessica looked around. "Clem's not here yet?"

"I didn't know he was supposed to be." Mrs. Fletcher's mouth settled into a straight line and she threw Jessica a sharp look.

Creight stood inside the door, his frown deepening into a scowl at the obvious setup.

"Guess he's running a bit late." Jessica shivered with cold and rubbed her arms. "Do I smell coffee? Oh, that sounds good. It's so cold outside!"

Mrs. Fletcher pointed to the round dining room table. "Have a seat." She was annoyed at Jessica's second attempt at matchmaking and banged the cups and saucers as she moved about the kitchen.

Creight sat on the edge of his chair growing more peevish. "I can talk with Clem later." He began to rise to his feet.

Jessica placed a hand on his shoulder and gently pushed him back down. She leaned in and whispered. "She's bringing us coffee. You'll hurt her feelings if you leave now."

His scowl shifted to disbelief. "I don't know her well enough to hurt her feelings. And I don't like —"

Mrs. Fletcher came to the dining table and placed the coffee cups down.

Jessica lifted the cup and smiled. "Just what we need, isn't it Mr. Creight? You're not going to join us?"

"I just had mine." Mrs. Fletcher sat primly with her hands folded in her lap and her lips pursed.

Abe took a polite sip, set the cup back down, and fixed his eyes on the table.

Jessica filled the silence and awkwardness with talk about how Eugene and Edna spent three days in Chicago and then drove to Iowa to visit Edna's family for a few weeks. And how Jimmy and Gladys took the train to St. Louis for their honeymoon and spent five days seeing a play and going to a concert and doing some shopping. When the lull persisted, she smacked her forehead. "Oh! I just remembered. Clem's helping Donny with something. I'll just run over there and let him know we're here."

After a minute of uncomfortable silence, Creight stood. "If you'll just show me the back gate, I'll take a look at it. I can talk to Clem later."

Mrs. Fletcher also stood. "I don't *have* a back gate." She shot him a disapproving look as if the visit had been all his idea.

"Then why in the —" Creight shut his mouth and let out huff of annoyance. He would count to ten, lest he say something rude.

She crossed her arms. "A setup! That's what this is. And I don't like it. Not one bit."

"I sure as heck don't either. I'm a practical man and have no time for such nonsense. I'll take my leave."

"Perhaps that's best."

"Goodbye, then."

"Goodbye." Mrs. Fletcher walked him to the door and locked her hands in front of her.

Chapter 5

෬

Gabriel ran to The Red String Curio Store after school, eager to discuss the idea of the raffle with Mr. G.

When he walked inside, he greeted the trio of Dusty, Junior, and Henry gathered around a game of checkers.

"Afternoon, Gabriel!" said Henry.

"Guess what? We might move to a house. With a big yard and a treehouse."

Henry gave a distracted response. "Well, now, that is news indeed. I'm afraid these two are at a bit of an impasse." All three of the older men kept their eyes on the checkerboard.

Gabriel took off his coat and hung it behind the counter. Then he slipped on his green apron and went to the men's clothing shelves. He picked up the bowler, twirled it around on his finger, and placed it on his head. "Might be needing this," he said to himself.

Mr. G popped around to the counter and gestured down an aisle. "I'll leave them to it for a moment. Husband and wife. Young. Involving an oak vanity set."

"Guess what, Mr. G? We might get a new home. With a big treehouse!"

"A new home? Well, I hope it's not too far away. So!" he exclaimed, tapping the brim of the bowler. "Any more ideas? I told the boys about your idea for Valentine's Day."

None of "the boys" showed any interest in the topic and leaned in further for Dusty's next move.

"Here's what I have so far. We'll gather all the stuff that might sell for Valentine's Day and display it up front. I'll get Billy to help me. Next, we decorate – you know, put some signs in the windows, string some red paper hearts around the shop. Mom made some and they look really cheerful."

"Good, good." Mr. G smiled at the suggestions, though, except for the paper hearts, it was what he did every year anyway.

"And then –" Gabriel bookmarked his hands for dramatic effect "– right at closing, after everyone is done shopping, we'll have" – his arms opened wide – "a raffle!"

"A raffle! Hmm." Mr. G rubbed his chin in thought. "I've never done that before. I suppose I could round up an appropriate item or two." He nodded his head to one side and the other. "I must say, I rather like the idea. The build-up, the excitement." His face shifted to doubt. "Of course, it would only be effective if there was a crowd. And the way things have been going..."

"Leave that to me. I'll come up with something."

The little bell rang and Billy waved from the door. "Hi, Gabriel! Afternoon, Mr. G."

"Greetings, master Wilhelm!" said Mr. G. "Fare thee well?"

"Well enough. And thou-self? Did Gabriel tell you about the treehouse? When he moves, we're going to take turns visiting each other." He plopped down in the armchair near the group of men. "Hiya, fellas."

They murmured their hellos, eyes on the board.

"Who's winning?"

"Maybe no one," said Henry. "Hard to say."

"Hey, Billy," said Gabriel. "You'll help, won't you?"

"Sure! With what?"

"Fill him in, Gabriel. Let me tend to my customers and we'll strategize further, anon." Mr. G disappeared into the labyrinth and could be heard discussing the vanity set with the young couple.

Gabriel pulled up a wooden chair, straddled it backwards, and leaned in confidentially to Billy. "Business is slow. Mr. G needs help bringing some life and excitement into the Red String. So, we're going to have a Valentine's Day celebration. Fill the place up. You in?"

"Sure. I'll stand outside and grab people as they walk by. Bring 'em inside. What else?"

Gabriel took a large notepad from the counter and flipped through his pocket notebook. "We need to organize the ideas. I'll tell you what I have so far."

"You read, I'll write it down," said Billy, reaching for the notepad. "I know all about this stuff. We're learning how to outline in English class. You start with Roman numerals and capital letters and work your way down to little numbers and letters. It's kind of fun."

Billy read aloud as he wrote: "Valentine's Day at The Red String Curio Store. Roman numeral one. Fill store. Capital A. Pull people inside." He showed it to Gabriel.

"Good, Billy. That looks official. Two. Decorate the place. Tommy and Amy and Mickey will help with that. Three. You and I will search the store for anything to do with love."

Billy wrote it down but looked up, doubtful. "That's impossible. Everybody loves something different." He gestured to various items around the store. "Some people love the globes, others love books, some people love those old doorstops like that Aladdin's lamp over there, and –"

"No, I mean – you know, like Valentine's Day love."

"Romantic love," Junior clarified, pulling on his long gray beard.

Billy gave it some thought. "Huh. So, what will we look for?"

"Well, …" Gabriel drew a blank. "What do you think, Henry? What *do* we look for?"

Henry leaned back and tapped his tented his fingers together. "Let's see. Start with the obvious. Hearts. Cupids. Lovers."

"Roman numeral three. Find merchandise. Capital A. Search store. B. Love stuff." Billy listed the items below by small numbers and smiled proudly at the details of his list.

The theme caught Dusty's attention and he added his two cents. "It's primarily a ladies' holiday. You could look for lace and mirrors, jewelry, decorative boxes."

"C. Ladies things," said Billy, and numbered the various items. "Might as well add this: D. Girl stuff. 1. Jump ropes. 2. Dolls. 3. – should I include marbles?"

Henry, Junior, and Dusty exchanged glances.

"Mature love," Dusty clarified.

Billy nodded: "Got it. E. Mature love. 1. Old people. Maybe that should go up here. No, here." He circled that category and drew an arrow to where it should be inserted.

"Perhaps," said Henry, "you could check with Mr. G about the items."

They paused in their conversation while Mr. G rang up the sale for the vanity set and discussed delivery.

The young woman stood on her toes and kissed her husband's cheek. "I love it, John. It will look so pretty in our bedroom."

Junior pointed his head at the couple. "That kind of love."

"Ohhh," said Billy. "*Now* I get it." Under III-E-2, he wrote: Mushy stuff.

When the couple left, Mr. G joined the group, dropping onto a wooden chair. "Only my second sale of the day. Thank goodness it was a large one."

"This game is going nowhere," Dusty said. "Stalemate?"

"Stalemate," said Junior, and they stacked the pieces and placed them in the checker box.

Henry kicked into gear. "So, Mr. G, this Valentine's Day celebration. What's the plan? Gabriel and Billy will round up merchandise. How can we three help? We can do more than sit around taking up space in your shop."

Mr. G let out a deep sigh. "I'm not sure there's much we can do to increase business this time of year, but it's certainly worth a try."

"Did I hear mention of a raffle?" asked Junior. "How about a framed poem, like we did for Christmas? Love-themed, of course. The noblest of sentiments."

"In your artistic calligraphy. That's a fine idea. I'll select a few frames you can choose from. I thank you, Junior." Mr. G hooked his thumbs under his red suspenders, imagining the event. "I suppose I could set up a small table by the window and offer cookies. Assuming people will wander in."

Billy added: IV. Raffle, A. Junior, poems. V. Snacks. A. Table by window. 1. Cookies.

"That's where *I* can help," said Henry, growing animated. "You leave the refreshments to me and Martha."

Billy added that information to his growing outline.

Dusty, not wanting to be outdone, immediately thought of his late wife's famous punch. "And I'll arrange the beverage. Juniper's recipe. Also known as 'Pepper's Punch.' She'll be smiling down to know that it's still being enjoyed."

"Pepper in punch?" Billy looked up from his notetaking.

Dusty shook his head and smiled. "That's a nickname for Juniper – Pepper. Along with June, Juney." He leaned back in his chair. "But I always thought Pepper suited her. She was a vibrant, energetic person. Added a bit of spice to life."

"That she did," said Mr. G. He turned to Gabriel and Billy. "She and my wife were friends, you know. That was long years ago." He looked over at Dusty. "I think they would have enjoyed this little Valentine's Day event we're planning."

"Indeed! They would have run circles around us. Had the whole thing planned down to the smallest detail."

Mr. G laughed in agreement. "As it is, it's fast taking shape. I hope I have enough appropriate merchandise for sale. Junior, how quickly can you work? We might as well make a display of other poems. I certainly have enough frames. They sold like hotcakes over Christmas."

"My fingers are stiff, but my heart's afire. I write at a pretty good clip, once I'm inspired." Junior pushed himself to his feet. "I'll choose some of the favorites. He struck a poet's pose with outstretched arm, and spoke in the light Scots dialect of Robert Burns. 'O my Luve is like a red, red rose, that's newly sprung in June.'" He placed his hand on his chest, and shifted to softer tone. "'How do I love thee? Let me count the ways.' Short poems, to the point. So they fit in the frames."

"Ah, the Brownings," said Dusty, drawing on his professorial days. "How about that exceedingly short poem by Robert? That would fit in the smallest of frames. And might be a good seller," he added with a snicker.

"Which poem is that?" Henry asked.

Junior smiled. "'Rhyme for a Child Viewing a Naked Venus in a Painting of *The Judgement of Paris*.' A mouthful of a title if ever there was one." He pulled on his beard as he imagined it in a frame. "It might do. I'd have to use a small script for that title."

"And the poem itself?" asked Henry.

"Short." Junior's tone shifted to amusement as he recited: "He gazed and gazed and gazed and gazed, Amazed, amazed, amazed, amazed."

Billy raised his head from his outline and looked from Junior to Dusty to Mr. G to Henry, wondering at their chuckles. "What was so amazing?"

"And on that note..." Junior put on his hat and flexed his fingers. "I'd better get busy." He tipped his hat. "Gentleman."

"Best be going, too," said Henry. "Martha might need a hand with dinner."

"And me," said Dusty, rising to his feet. "Need to locate that recipe, make a list of ingredients."

"Thank you, all," said Mr. G. "At the very least, we'll have ourselves a little party. Gabriel and Billy can join me as hosts for the event."

"Hosts!" Billy cried, grinning as he added another category.

"I could even play a few songs," continued Mr. G, "seeing that the old upright has been tuned."

"Music!" cried Gabriel. "Add that, Billy. Mom said they always had music at her work parties."

"Holy mackerel," muttered Billy. "This thing is getting long."

When the clock behind the counter struck 5:00, Billy let out a groan of relief and set his outline down. "We can finish this tomorrow. Gotta go!" He ran for the door. "See you later. Bye, Mr. G."

"Well, Gabriel, this is turning into a rather entertaining notion. Sales or no sales, we'll enjoy ourselves. Have our own celebration. Amongst friends. After all, friendship is a sort of love, isn't it?"

Mr. G began to tidy the checkers circle, as they called it, of three stuffed chairs, an old leather wing-back, and a few wooden chairs gathered around a low table.

Gabriel's face scrunched in worry. "Mr. G, it's almost time to go and I didn't do any work yet!" He lifted two pillows from the armchairs and hit them together, plumping them up.

"Of course, you did. You get paid for thinking, too."

Gabriel laughed at the idea. "Still, I want to do some *work* work."

"In that case, how about we locate a few of the folding tables and wipe them down. We'll need them for the merchandise you'll be gathering."

An hour later, when Mr. G waved goodbye to Gabriel and flipped the sign in the door to "Closed," Gabriel felt that his plan was already succeeding. Mr. G was happier.

Chapter 6

On a cold February evening, Kate sat in the living room with her children. Ursula brought mugs of hot chocolate and set them by Kate and Gladys, and went to the kitchen for Jessica's and her own. "I'll pour Paul's when he comes down."

Jimmy gave a light-hearted guffaw and held up a beer bottle. "Trust me, he's going to want one of these. You don't come back from war and sip on hot cocoa."

"Clem does," Jessica answered.

"He does that for you."

"Which I think is real sweet," said Gladys.

Kate set her sewing down and took a sip of her hot chocolate. "It's perfect, Ursula. Cozy."

Jimmy responded by taking another swig of beer and continuing their conversation. "Admit it, Jess. It was a disaster. If anything, you made it worse."

Jessica's mouth turned down in disappointment. "I should have had Clem with me. He would have smoothed things out, gotten them to talk about something. By the time he came back with me, Mr. Creight had already left." She winced as she remembered Mrs. Fletcher's words to her: "I want no more nonsense with that man. Back gate. Back door. I don't need his help. I've been fixing things around this house for years!"

Kate looked up from her sewing. "You tried. Your intentions were good." She bit off the thread, rethreaded the needle, and knotted it. "If you want to do some matchmaking, try with Paul."

"I'm working on it. Though there's no challenge there. He's clearly still sweet on Lucille."

Ursula smiled. "He always has been."

Gladys sipped her hot chocolate. "She always asks about him when she comes into Arnold's to shop. She thinks I have inside information."

"Paul and Lucille are one thing," Jimmy said, "but Creight and Mrs. Fletcher? Of all people. I don't know Mrs. Fletcher very well, but he's no picnic. Abe Creight, the 'practical man,' all business. Remember how he and Eugene –"

"I know, I know," said Jessica. "They quarreled over a piece of land. But they're friends now, aren't they, Ursula?"

"I believe so." Ursula reached over and stroked Frankie's hair. He had fallen asleep on the couch with his little wooden truck clasped in his hand. "Mr. Creight has a soft side to him. He's actually very kind. Sensitive, even."

"So is Mrs. Fletcher," Jessica said. "Once you get to know her."

"If you say so." Jimmy went to the radio to find some music.

"How would you describe Mrs. Fletcher, Mom?" asked Ursula. "I don't really know her, other than to say hello when I see her in town."

"That's because she keeps to herself so much." Kate set her sewing down and gave it some thought. "Well, she lost her husband at a young age. That can change a person. Martin was just a baby, so she raised him on her own. And then to lose him. Her only child. She's all alone now." She picked up her sewing and located her last stitch.

"Which is why..." Jessica left the obvious unsaid. "Two old people who have recently lost their sons."

Kate's head snapped up. "Old! What does that make me?"

"Forever young, Mom," said Ursula.

Kate smiled at the comment. "If only. But to finish my thought, I think Anne Fletcher is a good-hearted person. She's quick to respond to anyone who needs a helping hand." She made a few stitches and added, "Though she does have a reputation for being rather – prickly, shall we say? She's proud. And can be stubborn. Difficult, even, though –"

Paul came clomping down the stairs, his hair wet from the shower. "I heard 'proud,' 'stubborn,' and 'difficult.' Let me guess – talking about Creight?"

Except for Jessica, they all laughed. "That just proves my point," she said. "They have a lot in common."

"Can I bring you a hot chocolate?" Ursula asked Paul, going to the kitchen.

"How about a beer?" he hollered after her.

Jimmy smiled up at the ceiling but didn't say anything.

Ursula returned and handed the beer to Paul. "We were also just talking about Lucille."

Paul lifted the bottle and took a drink, and then looked over at Jimmy. "Turn that up! That's a good song."

Ursula traded a smile with Gladys at his evasion, and gently lifted Frankie. "I'm going to take him upstairs. Turn it up as loud as you want. You know he can sleep through anything."

Jimmy pulled Gladys to her feet. "May I have this dance?" He exaggerated dancing cheek to cheek with her, causing Gladys, and the others, to laugh.

*

Jessica went on weaving together the lives of the two lonely people, against their wills, and against the advice of everyone.

She paid a visit to Mrs. Fletcher, ostensibly to apologize.

Once they were seated with a cup of tea, Jessica brought up the subject of Abe Creight.

"I'm sorry about that. I truly am. It's just that — well, you know Ursula has befriended him. She and his son Jeremy were classmates." She slowly shook her head. "Ursula worries about him. She thinks he isn't eating properly. Since, you know…"

"I do know. Very well. There's many a time I have no appetite but I make myself eat something."

Jessica knitted her brow, deep in thought. "I thought he looked so lean. He's a strong man, but I'm sure he's lost weight."

A flash of guilt crossed Mrs. Fletcher's face. "I would have been more than happy to feed him. Had he stayed. Of course, I would. I just don't want anyone, including you, to be feeling sorry for me. Or worse, to be getting any ideas."

Jessica made a show of almost choking on her tea. "Of course not! But you know, he did seem somewhat happy at the wedding, which surprised us all. I think it did him good to get out, to mix with people. Ursula wishes he would go to the Valentine's Day dance. But I'm sure he'll say no. Which is a shame. It would be good for him."

"You can't force people to do something they don't want to do. Especially someone as proud and stubborn as Abe Creight."

At those words, Jessica truly choked on her tea and tried to hide her smile.

Mrs. Fletcher fixed her with a stern look. "I knew him in school. I've known him for a long time. He was always that way. A loner. Now his wife, Anita, was another story. A good woman. A shame he lost her."

Jessica nodded. "Mom says loss is very hard and can change a person."

"It is. It does. But life goes on, doesn't it? We must make the best of things."

Jessica could see that Mrs. Fletcher would not allow one ounce of pity for herself. She smiled into her tea as she imagined the older woman sitting up straight and declaring: "I'm a practical woman."

*

Jessica spotted Mr. Creight leaving the grocery store in town. "Your turn," she thought, and crossed the street.

When Creight saw her coming his way, he hurriedly loaded the box of goods into the cab of his truck, hoping to avoid her.

Jessica ran up to him. "Hi, Mr. Creight. Running errands? Sure has gotten colder, hasn't it?"

He made small sounds to her questions.

"I wanted to say that I'm sorry about the other day. By the time Clem and I got back to Mrs. Fletcher's, you had gone."

"I – I had things to do. I'm sure Clem can manage without my help."

"I guess he can always ask someone else if he gets stuck. I just thought Mrs. Fletcher would be more comfortable with you. You know, someone she knows. She said you were in school together."

"That was a long time ago. Well, I gotta –"

"Clem and I worry about Mrs. Fletcher." Jessica looked away as her face filled with concern. "Now that she's all alone."

Creight's face softened and he rubbed his foot on the pavement. "I have my daughters and grandkids, though they don't live close."

"You're fortunate. Martin was her only child. I was thinking – I just thought you might look in on her now and then. Help with minor repairs. That back door of hers sticks so. She's a very proud woman. Too proud to ask for help."

If he was honest with himself, that exchange with Anne Fletcher had been bothering him. The tone of anger between them. It was not his way. He gave it some thought. "I can look in on her from time to time. We were classmates, after all. It'd be the fitting thing to do."

"For the most part, she keeps to herself. She shops and runs errands, and helps out when asked. But she doesn't do anything for herself."

Creight stiffened at her words, fearing where she was heading.

Jessica gave a laugh at her silly notions. "I was even hoping she would help out at the Valentine's Day dance. Just to get out and mix with people. It would do her good, don't you think?"

Abe made a noncommittal sound and opened his truck door.

"When I was a little girl, I used to pick her flowers. I was scared of her back then, but now, with Clem, I've gotten to know her. She's really very kind. Warm even –"

"Need to be getting back. Say hello to Ursula for me."

"Oh – I'll be sure to. It's been nice talking with you, Mr. Creight." Jessica smiled and waved goodbye.

To herself, she said: "Two peas in a pod. They just don't know it yet."

*

Two days later, Abe Creight put his toolbox in the back of his truck and drove into town. He parked in front of Mrs. Fletcher's house, steeled himself for a possible battle, and walked up to the porch, holding a small conversation with himself. *She's all alone. Just be compassionate. Don't get riled up by her prickliness. Count to ten if you feel your anger rising.*

He knocked at her door. And tried to ignore the sour face that greeted him.

Mrs. Fletcher looked around to see if Clem or Jessica was with him. "Yes?" she snapped, her voice full of suspicion.

One, two, three, four... "Was in town anyway and thought I could look at that door. Jessica said it sticks."

She waited a few moments, deciding whether to shoo him away or say thank you. She looked him up and down. He did look thin.

"I'd appreciate it. It's almost lunch. I'll fix us a sandwich."

"No need for that."

"That's the only way I'll accept your help." She hadn't meant to sound so harsh.

Proud and prickly. One, two, three... "Fine. Show me the door."

"It's nothing really. Been meaning to buy a plane, to fix it myself."

"No need. Got one right here."

She showed him the back door, opened a step stool, and left him alone. Then she went into the kitchen and heated up a pan of soup and made several lunchmeat sandwiches.

Creight used the plane to shave a bit off the top of the door, sanded it, and ran his hand over it. He repeated it again and again, meticulous in his work. When he was satisfied, he opened and closed the door several times to make sure it shut properly. Then he tightened the door latch.

"Lunch is ready."

She stood before him with her hands folded. Dressed in a gray dress and a calico gray apron. Her gray hair in a tight bun at her neck.

Stern, thought Abe. *No wonder Jessica was afraid of her.*

"Door's fixed." Abe opened and closed the door to show her. "I'll be on my way then."

"You'll do no such thing. We had a deal, Abe Creight."

He nodded, regretting that he had agreed to lunch. What on earth would they talk about? "I'll just wash up." He held up his calloused farmer's hands and looked around.

"Down the hall. On the right."

Mrs. Fletcher didn't like the way she sounded. Martin was right, she thought. I do tend to bark out my sentences.

Abe looked slightly dismayed when he came to the table and saw a plate stacked high with sandwiches. He was used to eating lightly. Sometimes even forgot to eat.

"I don't eat much," he began to say.

"You're skin and bones!" Mrs. Fletcher ladled out a bowl of soup. "I expect you to eat what I made for you."

One, two, three, four, five, six... She sounds just like my daughters. Bossy!

She noted his expression and softened her tone. "Eat what you can. I'll wrap the rest for you. I imagine you don't cook much at home. It's hard to cook for one, isn't it?"

He took a spoonful of soup.

Mrs. Fletcher carefully watched his expression. Did he like it?

He ate the rest and tipped his bowl. "Mighty fine. Better than mine. What'd you put in there?"

"It's the herbs." She refilled his bowl and soon they were comparing tomato soup recipes.

She noticed that once he got talking, he ate freely, starting in on a second sandwich.

"Was hungrier than I thought. Guess it's the cold weather."

When she failed to convince him to have a third, she cleared their plates. "I won't force you, but I *am* going to wrap them for you to take home. Now, let me make some coffee."

He was about to object to both, but the look on her face told him to give it up. It would mean counting to fifty, and he had to admit, the sandwiches were good.

With the table cleared and their coffee before them, they once again became aware of the awkwardness of the situation. When they stirred milk into their cups, the clinking of spoons seemed to echo from wall to wall.

Creight felt the need to clear the air. He tried to think of how to approach the subject, and decided that simple and direct was best. Looking into his cup he said, "I apologize for my behavior the other day. I – I misread the situation."

"You read it as clearly as I did. It was a setup! Jessica's a good girl, but I told her to stop with that nonsense. Young people these days..." She shook her head.

"I suppose she meant well. Still, it's good you set her straight."

"I don't want to be rude, Abe, and I appreciate you fixing my door. But I was on my own with Martin for a good long time. I'm used to managing things on my own. For the most part, I can handle my own repairs. Don't go thinking that I'm a damsel in distress."

"Wouldn't dream of it," he said, suppressing a smile at *that* image. He took a sip of coffee and eyed the stack of wrapped sandwiches. "Likewise, I can cook my own meals. Been doing it for years."

Mrs. Fletcher stiffened her back. Several moments of silence followed.

The calming effect brought on by a good meal and two cups of coffee softened Creight's mood. Surprising even himself, he asked, "So, if I need a hand with plumbing, you're saying you could help?"

For the first time, Mrs. Fletcher allowed the hint of a smile. "I might. I cleaned the trap by myself in the fall."

"I'm impressed."

The good meal and gentle banter had a similar softening effect on her. "Though if I come and get my hands dirty, I'll expect a nice meal."

Creight chuckled. "Fair's fair. Might even make you my famous pork chops and parsnips. With apricots, if I can get them. Apples, if not."

Mrs. Fletcher's face registered distaste. "I'm not sure about *that*."

"Don't be so hasty. You might like it."

Mrs. Fletcher was not prepared to change her mind but remained silent.

"Course, I'd never have you help with plumbing. But I might trim the parlor after winter. How're you at painting?"

"I'm a perfectionist, as you might imagine."

Creight smiled as he finished his coffee, enjoying the exchange. No harm done, he thought. Just old schoolmates.

He soon said his goodbye. They both left with the satisfaction that they had made their point, and were not one to be pitied. Though Mrs. Fletcher also enjoyed the gratification that she had gotten some food into Creight.

For his part, Creight left with the feeling that he had done a good turn for the lonely woman, and relief that now Jessica would back off. And Anne Fletcher was not as bad as she made herself out to be. Was good, decent company. A practical woman. No nonsense about her. Without even thinking about it, Abe unwrapped a sandwich and enjoyed it on his drive home.

Chapter 7

❦

In a lively English pub, a small fireplace crackled and emitted enough heat to warm Izzy's feet and legs. She and Red had strolled through the village, and were now warming up over dinner.

Izzy had been in England, just outside of London, for almost a month now. Red worked long hours in the London office, processing mounds of paperwork for the GIs trying to get back home. She needed to stay busy, so she had signed up for various volunteer efforts. She spent most of her days at an orphanage that was close to the hospital where Red volunteered on nights and weekends. She and Red had taken many walks and talked about the war, the changes in their lives, and the predictions for the post-war world.

She came to know Red in a new way, watching him interact with the patients and townsfolk, seeing him in a new environment. Seeing him, for the first time, as a recovering patient, himself. His external injuries had healed for the most part. Though his leg and eyes occasionally bothered him, she knew it was the internal wounds that he still struggled with.

He was different. There were layers of impenetrable sadness in him. Little by little he shared a few memories and experiences that gave him pain. She never pushed him or asked too many questions, but let him relate events at the pace that felt right for him.

They recently talked about their so-called love lives. Red described his brief time with Myra and the ensuing falling apart of something that had never really been there. And the divorce.

Izzy touched upon some of the men she had spent time with, and how she had even considered marrying one of them. Archie. And how it was Lillian who had brought her to her senses and said the attraction was only because he looked like Red.

That conversation had led to small recriminations, then to all out blaming, then to a fiery raised-voiced argument.

They had avoided each other for two days. Then just when Izzy couldn't take it any longer, she hurried to his rooming house, only to bump into him on his way to see her.

Izzy embraced him. "I didn't come here to fight with you."

"I don't want to waste a single minute of my time with you, Izzy." Red held her as if he was never going to let go.

They walked along the stream, arms linked. They vented their anger and jealousy, and finally expressed the crippling pain behind the sense of betrayal – to know that someone else had enjoyed even a small bit of the person they loved. The fear that they had lost each other, and the depression that followed. And then the argument was buried and forgotten. They had no time to waste on what hadn't gone right in their lives. The war had taught them that. They were greedy for every moment of their time together.

They grew closer and closer and more entrenched in their love. And yet – neither of them brought up what the next step would be.

However, tonight Izzy decided to broach the subject. She had received a letter from Lillian, which included a note from Mr. Rockwell telling Izzy to come back or be fired.

Izzy sipped an ale as she listened to Red relate a humorous incident with one of the new patients who, despite his injuries, was a real practical joker.

Warmed by the meal and the glowing embers, Izzy told Red about the letter from Lillian.

"She couldn't be happier. Charles home, the boys doing well, and little Charlotte. Oh, you should see her, Red. She's the sweetest little baby. To see them all cooing around her warms the heart."

Red smiled at the image but remained silent. When he saw that Izzy expected a response, he said, "I'm happy for them. It was so good to see Charles the few times he came to London. He deserves to be happy."

Izzy watched his face. It was all shadowy with doubts and memories again, but she needed to make a decision.

She opened her purse and took out the envelope. "From my boss. His usual, charming self." She pushed it over for Red to read.

He scanned the letter, gave a soft laugh, and read aloud: "Need I remind you what the contract that *you* drafted stipulates? That an absence of over two months voids all terms and conditions. If you want to keep your job, be back by March! We're busier than ever."

Izzy folded her arms on the table. "Subtle, isn't he?"

Red handed the note back to her. "How do you feel about that? Do you want to go back?"

Izzy put the letter away and snapped her purse shut. "If and when I leave my job, I want it to be on my terms. Not because he's forced me out." She gave a huff of indignation.

"You've always loved your job. I know how much it means to you."

Izzy rested her chin in her hand. "If truth be told, I'm reluctant to give it up. I built that career, carved out that position for myself. I'm good at it. I've been able to save and I like that sense of security. I like making money. I like having a purpose. A reason to get up in the morning."

Red nodded as he listened to her. "I admire that about you."

Izzy watched him rub at his eyes, a new habit she had noticed. She never knew if it was his injuries, or if it was his way of pushing aside unwanted visions.

Red leaned back and gave a smile. "Well, give it some thought. You have a few weeks to decide."

He wanted to say that if he returned and worked at his family's business, they would have all the money they needed. She could stay at Rockwell's or not. If they were to be together. Instead, he paid the bill and rose to his feet.

"It's getting late. More snow is expected." He reached for her coat and held it out for her to slip her arms in.

When her back was to Red, Izzy sighed at his inadequate response. But she smiled when she faced him. She couldn't push the matter. It had to come from him.

He walked her to the house where she was renting a room. They made plans for the following day, kissed, and said goodnight. Izzy watched him leave, and closed the door behind her.

Before turning off her bedside lamp, Izzy reread the letter from Red that had prompted her decision to come to England. Though she knew the words by heart, to see them in his handwriting reached into her heart more deeply:

> *I have loved only you. That has never changed. I don't expect forgiveness ... I will always want the best for you, Izzy, and I hope that one day you will find love again.*

Had she misinterpreted his words? There was a finality woven into them – a sort of goodbye – which she saw only now. Wasn't there?

She read the words again. No, there was no mistaking his love for her. She turned off the lamp, and went over their time together since the day she arrived.

There had been moments of euphoria, moments of reliving and rediscovering their love. They had laughed and talked and danced, like old times. And yet.

It was different. They were different. Older. The war had changed them. It still hurt to think about it – that while recovering from being wounded, Red had rashly married his nurse. And shaken by the betrayal, she herself had almost leapt into a marriage. That wasn't who they were. It was as if they had been living inside a constantly shaken kaleidoscope world that was fragmented, dizzying, and ever-shifting.

Izzy rolled onto her side, the letter still in her hand. There was sadness in Red, a look of loss in his eyes that haunted her. Even when he smiled.

She knew Red well enough to know that, in his mind, he had done the unpardonable. Destroyed her trust, her belief in him. His belief in himself. That was it. Everything with Red was about honor. His comment about Charles deserving to be happy. As if he himself was not deserving.

If that was how he felt, then it was up to her to convince him. For in spite of everything that had happened, she knew that their love remained strong, pure, and untouchable. Perhaps it was even stronger now, having been tempered by the hard times. And she could think of no more worthy way to spend the rest of her life than in fighting for and protecting that love.

Chapter 8

∾

At The Red String Curio Store, plans were shaping up for the Valentine's Day party, as it was now called. Dusty, Junior, and Henry gathered around the checkers table and added their suggestions, while Billy wrote everything down. He had worked diligently on his outline and was impressed – if somewhat overwhelmed – by its complexity.

"Let's go over the list," said Mr. G. "Gabriel, how are you boys going to search for merchandise?"

"We figure we'll start at one side of the store and work our way to the other. Billy, read an example of the things we'll look for." He glanced down at Billy's outline. "Pick a short one."

Billy scanned the pages and thumped his finger on page three of his outline. "III-F-4-a: Items that are red or pink. A long list follows," he explained to the group. "G. Anything to do with Valentine's Day, like 3-b-ii: cupids – with and without bows and arrows." He looked up. "Maybe that should be sub-sub-sub category?" He shook off the notion. "H-1-a: Anything with flowers." He turned the list sideways to read the items in the margins. "c-i: especially roses. c-ii: violets. c-iii: daisies? We're not sure about those. I and J –"

"You're giving me a headache with that infernal outline," said Dusty. He scowled as Henry made a jump.

Billy rubbed his forehead. "You should try reading this thing! Do you want to hear more categories?"

"No!" came a unified answer from the group.

"I think you boys have the hang of it." Mr. G studied the large faded tapestries hanging on one of the brick walls. One showed a castle in the distance and mounted hunters in pursuit of a fleeing deer, another depicted a pastoral courtship. "Perhaps we can use those tapestries. Hang them behind the counter, to set the tone. They're full of themes of love. You see how that young swain offers his beloved a bundle of roses?" He gestured to the other tapestry. "And there we have the metaphor of the hunt."

Gabriel jerked his head back as he studied the hunters chasing down a wounded stag. "For Valentine's Day?"

"Yes, indeed," said Dusty, becoming interested in the conversation. "Echoing back to the courtly themes in medieval poetry wherein the stag hunt served as an allegory for the hunt for love."

"It doesn't seem very romantic," said Gabriel. "The other tapestry does. With a garden and a cottage."

Billy nodded in agreement. "Yep. And there are two birds on the branches above the swain guy and lady." He turned back to the medieval scene. "But I like the hunt picture better."

"Lovebirds!" cried Mr. G. "An excellent observation, Billy. Add that to your list. Lovebirds, doves, swans. All symbols of love."

Billy squeezed in the new category.

"How about bird cages?" Gabriel asked, glancing around the store.

"Possibly," said Mr. G. "Gather anything that might do and bring it to the table. Perhaps we can pair a few items together."

"That goes under Possible Merchandise." Billy wrote down the new item in a tiny scrawl at the bottom of the fourth page. "III-J-8-q-vi-rectangle: birdcage. Whew!"

The checkers game came to a halt as the group of men looked over at Billy.

"Rectangle?" asked Mr. G.

Billy nodded. "I had too many letters and numbers so I added shapes." He looked down at the mess of crossed out categories, numbers and letters, lines with arrows snaking their way through words, scribbles in the margins, and shapes. He groaned and looked up at Mr. G. "You think I can be done with this?"

Mr. G gave a firm nod. "I believe we're sufficiently established in our planning to dispense with the outline."

"Thank goodness. I couldn't have taken much more," groused Dusty, kicking himself for missing a jump.

"Me either." Billy smiled in relief. "Now we can get to the fun part. The hunt!"

"We set up two tables along the wall in the front," said Gabriel. "We'll bring everything there and arrange it all later."

"Mr. G," said Billy, "you said Gabriel and I will be hosts for the party. Maybe we should wear costumes to stand out, so people know to come to us for help. Not like Halloween costumes. Something simple, so we still look like us, just more partyish."

Mr. G smiled at the idea. "Good thinking. A celebratory touch. Something from the shop."

"I'll wear my bowler, for starters," said Gabriel. "It brings me luck."

"Also known as a Derby hat," Dusty said, trying to distract Henry from the double jump at hand.

"Perhaps one of the embroidered waistcoats," suggested Mr. G. "They would add a festive flair. Take a look in the men's clothing section. See what you like."

The little bell on the door rang and Mr. G went to greet the customer. "I'll leave you boys to it."

Billy and Gabriel went to the shelves of clothing and found a stack of colorful vests, cummerbunds, and various styles of neck cloths.

Gabriel held up a richly embroidered vest. "Here's a red one with squiggly flowers and vines. What do you think?" He slipped it on and looked in the standing mirror.

Billy nodded. "It goes with the hat." He pulled out an emerald green one and tried it on. "It's not pink or red, but I like it. It's kind of big. You think it's too long?"

Gabriel eyed the vest that reached Billy mid-thigh. "Not at all. It looks like a tunic. Mine's kind of long too. We're proper gentl'men, Billy," he added with a wag of his head.

"Oi say," Billy said, slipping into character. "Tut tut and talley-ho and all 'at."

They looked at each other in the mirror, trying out their new personas. They stuck out their stomachs, hands behind their back, and strutted around.

Gabriel tried out the leer from the pirate Toby mug, and their laughter increased as their impersonations grew more outlandish. They added several years to their characters, Billy pulling on an imaginary beard and becoming hard of hearing. Gabriel grabbed a cane and stumbled about, bumping into the mirror and saying to his reflection, "beggin' your pardon, sir."

"Mustaches!" said Billy. "We'll draw on mustaches, maybe a goatee."

"Come on. Let's start searching for stuff."

Billy and Gabriel were soon combing through the merchandise. After a little hesitation and doubt about what might be appropriate, they gathered item after item, running them by each other and then stacking them on the tables.

Gabriel lifted a small white heart-shaped bowl, trimmed in gold. "This is perfect."

"Here's a red book," said Billy. "And here's one of those fat babies with wings."

Gabriel lifted a small porcelain statue and turned it around in his hand. "Here are two crows – do you think that counts?"

"Sure. Mr. G said to include birds. This is like a treasure hunt!"

They gathered figurines and filigree mirrors, tea pots and cups with roses, red buttons and a pink pin cushion, ruby-tinted wine goblets, two pink piggy banks, and anything with flowers, birds, and hunters. They found a wide depiction of romantic couples – on sheet music and book covers, on old postcards and framed pictures – and an assortment of lamps, bookends, footstools, placemats, and vases that, to their minds, had a touch of the romantic about them.

"Gosh," said Gabriel, inspecting the mound of items. "There's love stuff everywhere, once you start looking for it."

"Gabriel!" cried Billy. "Look what I found!"

Gabriel spun around. "Where'd you go?" He looked down one aisle, then around another. "Where are you, Billy?"

"In the back!"

Gabriel wound his way through the aisles and found Billy standing proudly with his find – an old leather quiver with a few dusty arrows whose feathers were either crushed or missing altogether.

"The hunt!"

"Nice find, Billy. It'll go with those cupids."

Billy took out the arrows and inspected them. "The points are gone, but you can't tell when – Hey!" His eyes flashed in excitement. "I just re-membered something I saw. I'll be right back." He dashed off and was gone for a few seconds. When he returned, he was wearing a green felt hat.

"It matches your vest!" said Gabriel.

"It even has a green feather!" Billy slung the quiver over his shoulder, and smoothed down the long emerald waistcoat. Then he turned around with a proud smile.

Gabriel widened his eyes at the impressive transformation.

"Robin Hood!" Billy said. "Let's go show Mr. G." Billy took off running. Gabriel followed him, glancing at items along the way.

They ran down the aisle, turned left, went down another row of shelves, paused, turned left – and found themselves back where they started.

"Maybe you should lead," said Billy. "You know the store better than I do."

"Follow me," said Gabriel. After several more turns they ended up at the counter.

"We got our costumes, Mr. G. What do you think?"

Mr. G hooked his thumbs under his suspenders. "Well! You certainly look festive."

"Red and green?" asked Junior skeptically.

Dusty looked up and frowned. "You look like Robin Hood."

"Thanks. I am!"

"But – for Valentine's Day?"

"Sure! It's the hunt," said Billy. "Like Mr. G said."

"With Cupid's arrows," added Gabriel, pointing to the quiver.

Gabriel saw a regular customer, Mrs. Jenkins, at one of the glass display cases.

"Hi, Mrs. Jenkins. What do you think of our costumes?"

"Why, look at you! I think you both look marvelous. For the Valentine's Day party? I couldn't help but overhear."

The little bell rang and Tommy and Mickey came in and greeted the group.

"Hi, Mr. G," said Tommy. "Gabriel told us about the party. We want to help. So does Amy. She's going to help Mom make strings of paper hearts and anything else you need."

"Wonderful!" said Mr. G. "We'll hang them in the window and along the counters."

"I've got refreshments under control," said Henry, taking a jump.

"I've got the punch," said Dusty, also taking a jump.

"I'm working on the poems," said Junior.

"Now all we need are shoppers to stop by!"

"I'll work on that," said Gabriel. "I'll tell our customers, for starters. You'll come, won't you, Mrs. Jenkins?"

"I wouldn't miss it for the world! And as luck would have it, my niece is visiting. She's about your age."

Tommy motioned to Henry and Gabriel. "We can spread the word at the hospital. There's a bunch of GIs who come in just for treatment. Some of them will stop by if we ask them."

"My dad can announce it at the next Scouts meeting," said Mickey. "We'll make sure it's crowded."

Mr. G nodded, but a look of concern crossed his face. "Hmm."

"What is it Mr. G?" Gabriel asked.

"Can't quite put my finger on it. Something at the back of my mind. "GIs. Boy Scouts…" He looked out at Gabriel and Billy, and Tommy and Mickey. And then over at Henry, Dusty, and Junior. "Aha. That's it."

They all turned from one to another in perplexity.

"I'd say we're a little heavy on the masculine element. Especially for a Valentine's Day party."

Henry looked at the others and hooted. "Right you are, Mr. G."

"Mom will come," offered Tommy.

"So will my mom," said Mickey.

"And Mrs. Jenkins and her niece."

"Martha will be here, of course," added Henry.

"Amy will be here and she'll bring her mom," said Tommy. "And Mrs. Wilson and Mrs. Mancetti will come if we ask them."

Dusty and Junior, two old loners, looked at each other, waiting to see how the other might contribute.

"I'll mention it to a few friends," said Junior.

"And what friends might those be?" Dusty asked.

"That woman – at the counter of the smoke shop. Mrs. Something-or-other."

Dusty looked at him dubiously.

Billy had been counting on his fingers. "That's ten ladies or so. Is that enough?"

Gabriel walked up to Mrs. Jenkins. "Could you bring your sister Harriet? She likes to shop here now and then."

"I'll do better that that! I'll have Harriet invite her ladies' club – the 'bluestocking club' as my husband likes to call it. Teachers and librarians for the most part."

Dusty and Junior nodded in approval.

"That would be splendid!" said Mr. G. "We'll be sure to have plenty of seating for them near the refreshment table."

"How exciting," said Mrs. Jenkins. "I was telling Mr. Jenkins that we should do something special this year. We'll come here for the party, and then go out to dinner with my niece. For now, Mr. G, I'll take this little brooch."

Mr. G rang her up and walked her to the door, thanking her, and then he joined the others.

"We could put some signs in the window," said Gabriel. "And mention all the things people can find here. Encourage them to come in."

"Excellent idea," said Mr. G. "Something like 'Join The Red String Curio Store for Valentine's Day." He turned to the group. "How about some slogans, gentlemen?"

Billy picked up his notebook, ready to write. "Don't worry, Dusty. I'll just jot down our ideas. I won't even number them."

"Search for your heart's content," offered Junior.

"Gifts for your mom and sisters," said Mickey.

"And sweetheart," added Tommy, and then blushed at his words.

Billy jotted down their slogans as quickly as they came. Then, inspired by the quiver of arrows, he looked up and smiled. "Happy hunting at The Red String Curio Store!"

Henry gave a hearty chuckle. "That's a doozy, Billy."

"We can draw a big picture of a bow and arrow, maybe a gun. 'Fun and adventure at the Red String!'" Billy added.

Mr. G tipped his head from side to side. "Yes, well, and of course, something about love and hearts."

"Bow and arrows? A gun!" Dusty objected, with a frown. "Please, keep it to hearts and cupids. 'Hearts galore!' 'Only hearts!'"

"As opposed to 'Lonely Hearts,'" Henry said with a chuckle.

"Ah, yes. Lonely Hearts," said Mr. G. "I understand those clubs are more popular than ever. Now that the war is over. Time to get on with life."

Dusty nodded. "I've seen those magazines for the matrimonially inclined. 'Cupid's column' giving advice for the lovelorn. Opportunities to correspond with like-minded seekers."

"You seem to be well-informed on the subject," Junior said, with a mischievous glint in his eye.

Dusty bristled at the insinuation. "It's common knowledge. Everyone's talking about them."

Henry smiled at the antagonism between the two men. "Now, now. There's nothing wrong with companionship. My life has been enriched a hundredfold since meeting Martha."

"I heard some of the patients talking about Lonely Hearts clubs at the hospital. What are they?" asked Gabriel.

Dusty and Junior looked at each other and then to Mr. G to answer the question.

"They're a kind of pen pal club. Where people can get to know one another." He clapped his hands with energy. "Now. Do we have enough catchphrases for the signs?"

"We have a lot," said Billy, underlining his 'Happy Hunting' slogan, "but we'll come up with some more."

"Don't forget to mention the raffle," said Junior. He leaned on his cane and pushed himself to his feet. "Until tomorrow," he said, tipping his hat.

Tommy, Mickey, and Billy also prepared to leave.

Mr. G jumped up to help a young couple with the purchase of a set of old books. "I'll finish up here, Gabriel. You go ahead and leave with the others."

"Thanks, Mr. G." Gabriel grabbed his coat and joined the others. As the boys walked back home, they went over their plans.

"Sounds like everything is in place," said Mickey. "We'll get started on the posters over the weekend."

"Come to our house on Saturday," Tommy suggested. "I'll tell Amy."

"And customers," said Gabriel. "We have to work on getting customers to come."

"I'll tell Mom to let all the neighbors know," said Mickey.

"Henry and I will be at the hospital tomorrow," said Tommy, "and can tell the nurses and visitors."

Gabriel grew hopeful. "And Billy and I will stand outside and wave people inside. In our costumes."

"Right," said Billy. "I'll stand at the door and yell, 'Come one, come all!'"

Mickey playfully swatted Billy's cap. "That sounds too much like a circus."

"How about 'Hear ye, Hear ye?' I could ring a bell. What do you think, Gabriel?"

"Sure! Let's try everything and see what works."

*

Later that night, almost asleep, Gabriel's thoughts about The Red String Curio Store blended with the houses and neighborhoods Charles had described over dinner.

"Hey, Tommy! I just thought of something. If we move, how will I get to my job?"

"The same way I'll get to my job. You won't."

Gabriel gave it some thought. "Dad said I can get a bike. Maybe I could ride it to work."

"It's going to be too far. Dad might have to get a car to get to his job. Mom will have to take a bus or train to come into the city. You and I will have to find new jobs. We might live in a place where there aren't any."

Gabriel was quiet for a few moments. "Will we have to go to a different school?"

"Of course, we will. But don't forget – we'll have all that other stuff. A big house, a big yard and –" Tommy punched up his pillow and rolled over facing the wall.

Nothing more was said about the move. Gabriel fell asleep with images in his mind of him taking a bus or train into Manhattan, or pulling up his new bicycle in front of The Red String Curio Store.

Chapter 9

❧

"I'm not joking this time," Jessica said to Paul. "Lucille just came out of the post office and is walking over by the dime store. Ursula, tell him."

Ursula nodded. "She is. She's standing in front of the window looking at the Valentine's Day display."

"The perfect setting." Jessica gave him a nudge. "Now's your chance. Go ask her to the dance."

When he hesitated, Ursula asked gently, "Do you want us to go with you?"

"What do you think I am – six years old?" He shoved his hands in his pockets and crossed the street. He approached Lucille as if he had just come upon her by chance.

"Hi, Lucille. Doing some shopping?"

"Hello, Paul. Just running some errands for Mom. You?"

"Ursula and Jessica have a few things to do so I drove them into town. I'm glad I ran into you. There's something I've been meaning to ask you."

She arched her eyebrows. "Oh, really? Now that you've just bumped into me you realize you have something to ask? Because you've been back for over a month now and have had very little to say to me. You've only called on me once!" As she waited for him to respond, her tone shifted from angry to hurt. "I thought after all those letters we exchanged I might expect a little more than that."

Paul looked everywhere but at Lucille. "I've been busy."

"So I've heard." She crossed her arms. "So, what did you want to ask me?"

Paul looked at her now and almost lost his nerve. "I was wondering if you'd care to go to the Valentine's Day dance with me?"

"The dance is next week and you're just asking me now? Couldn't you find anyone else?"

"I didn't ask anyone else! I'm asking you."

"Well, you waited too long. I'm already going." She whipped around and strode away.

Paul stared after her. Then he muttered to himself and kicked at the snow.

Jessica had been watching and now walked up to Paul. "Well?"

"Mind your own dang business!"

Ursula came up just in time to see him storm off. She looked at Jessica for an explanation.

Jessica smiled and gave a shake of her head. "Well matched, if you ask me."

"You better let him manage on his own, Jessica —"

"Oh, look, there's Mrs. Fletcher. I have to ask her something."

Ursula let out a groan. "Whatever you do, don't ask her about Mr. Creight." Ursula hurried to keep up, thinking that Jessica's matchmaking was exhausting.

"Hi, Mrs. Fletcher," said Jessica. "I was going to stop by to see you."

"Hello, Jessica, Ursula. I was hoping to see you, as well. You'll both be pleased to know that Abe Creight stopped by to fix my door – though that was completely unnecessary – but I managed to get some food into him. He does look a bit lean."

"We're so glad to hear that, aren't we?" Jessica turned to Ursula with a grin of triumph.

"Yes. Of course."

"Ursula brings him food now and then. But you know how proud he is. She always makes it look like it would just go to waste if he didn't accept it."

"Proud? I'd call that man stubborn! Still, we were classmates and he's on his own now. You have to make allowances for that. I told him from now on I can take care of my own repairs. Now, you have something you want to tell me?"

Jessica ignored the hint of a smile on Ursula's lips and forged ahead with her plan. "I was wondering if you'll be coming to the Valentine's Day dance." Before Mrs. Fletcher could decline, Jessica continued. "Because we still need a few people to help with serving. I'm on the refreshment committee."

"I wasn't planning on attending."

"We're going all out for the boys in uniform. Thankfully, out of uniform, now."

Mrs. Fletcher nodded. "I'd be happy to bake some cookies if that would help."

Jessica smiled politely. "That would be real nice. Ed and Opal are going to man the table later, and if we can't find anyone else, Mrs. Bloomfield will help out. But she's going to be busy with everything else." Jessica gave it some thought. "I guess Clem and I could tear ourselves away and serve for a while. I hate to miss out on the dancing, but it would just be for an hour or so in the beginning."

"I'm not much one for gatherings," Mrs. Fletcher said. "But if you can't find anyone else, I suppose I could come for an hour."

"All right. I'll let you know."

After they said their goodbyes, Ursula turned to Jessica. "Refreshment committee?"

"I *am* helping Sue Ellen with some ideas." She looked in the dime store window and smiled at the display of red and pink. "I need to pick up some valentines' supplies for my students." With a satisfied smile at her success with Mrs. Fletcher, Jessica opened the door for Ursula.

*

Paul and Ursula, allies of sorts, stayed up late in the living room talking after everyone else had gone to bed. Ursula had confided in him about Friedrich, and Paul now regularly asked her if she had received any news.

Jimmy and Eugene also asked after Friedrich, but only if no one else was around. It was still an awkward subject. She feared that Eugene would always have a visceral dislike of Germans, though he did his best not to show it. Besides, both brothers were completely absorbed with their new marriages. Ursula didn't want to put a damper on their newfound happiness, and she did her best to hide the dread she felt at Friedrich's imminent departure.

But Paul was different. She could freely speak to him about her feelings. She had told him about the few letters she had received from Friedrich from Camp Shanks, how worried she was about what was up ahead for him, and how helpless she felt. And now that she hadn't had a letter for over two weeks, her fear that he had already shipped out.

"I sure hope you hear from him soon." He sat on the couch with a concerned expression. "Strange to think that's what awaits him. A prison camp and forced labor." He let out a groan and rubbed his face. "I can't tell you how happy I am to be home. And the war over. I had it easy compared to a lot of guys." They sat in silence as they became lost in their own thoughts. Then Paul looked over at Ursula.

"I know how important letters are. You know, Lucille and I wrote a lot to each other while I was in the Pacific."

Ursula looked up, surprised. "You were not one for writing letters, as I remember. Lucille was an exception?"

He nodded in memory. "I got a lot of letters from other girls, my classmates and friends. But my correspondence with Lucille was different."

"Different how?"

Paul shifted in his chair and reached for the pillow beside him, needing to occupy his hands as he spoke. "It started off the same as with the others. How are you? What's the news from home? All the surface stuff. That's all we wanted to hear about. But then... I had kind of a dark period."

"What do you mean, Paul? Were you injured?"

He stopped turning the pillow around and stared at it on his lap. "No. But I saw some stuff. I was in the middle of some awful fighting for a while. And Lucille was the only one I wrote to about what I was going through."

"Not me or Mom? Or Jessica?"

"No. I didn't want you to know. I wanted you all to think of me as the same guy I was when I left. I needed that. I didn't want the family to be touched by my stuff. You all had enough to deal with when Francie was killed."

Ursula peered at her little brother, seeing a different side to him.

"Little by little, I started to share things with Lucille. We got kind of close through our letters. But when I came back, I didn't want all that. I wanted laughter and fun." He tossed the pillow up and caught it, and then rested it on his lap again. "I think I hurt her by ignoring her. But all that lighthearted surface stuff seems pretty empty after a while, you know? I miss her. That closeness."

Ursula smiled over at him. "It's understandable that you would need lightness. Lucille would understand that, if you spoke to her about it."

"I think I blew my chance. I was going to talk to her. That's what I wanted. I asked her to the dance, but she's already going with someone else."

"That doesn't mean anything. You should still talk to her. Tell her how you feel."

"The thing is —" Paul looked down at his hands and his voice almost broke. "The thing is – I love her. I told her that in the letters. And she said the same. We didn't talk about getting married or anything like that. We didn't talk about the future at all. We weren't sure there would be one."

"Oh, Paul." Ursula reached over and squeezed his arm. "All the more reason to speak to her now. I think she must be terribly hurt."

"I've been thinking the same thing. What worries me – terrifies me – is not knowing. I don't know if she still feels the same. I don't think I could stand it if she didn't. Maybe she just said those things to get me through a hard time."

Ursula gave a sad smile. "You made it through a war, Paul. You can make it through a conversation with Lucille."

Paul gave a laugh. "You're right. I'll wait until after the dance. I don't want to get in the way of – of anything."

"Don't wait too long." She stood and placed a hand on Paul's shoulder.

"Thanks, sis. Thanks for listening. I should have talked to you earlier. Maybe she'd be my date for the dance if I had."

Ursula climbed the stairs thinking that perhaps Jessica was right after all. People did need a little help, a little coaxing out of their isolation, a sympathetic ear. By Jessica pushing Paul to ask Lucille to the dance, it had at least brought the issue out in the open. At least Paul knew what he had to do now.

And Jessica's meddling had at least gotten Mr. Creight and Mrs. Fletcher on better terms with each other. Speaking terms. He fixed her door, she fed him. That was something. Friendship was important. She hoped Jessica would leave it at that. Still...

Maybe she would bake some bread tomorrow and bring it to Mr. Creight. She could mention the dance and tell him that it would make her happy if he would be there. It would be good for him to get out, to be around people.

Ursula had to laugh at herself. It was the very same advice that her mother always gave to her. And where matters of the heart were concerned, her mother was never wrong.

Chapter 10

∽

On the nights that Lillian volunteered at the hospital with Tommy and Gabriel, she brought Charlotte to Mrs. Kuntzman's home. It made Lillian happy to know that Charlotte was enjoying the grandmotherly love of their old babysitter.

Lillian and the boys now walked from the bus stop, along with Henry, talking about the patients who were leaving and the new ones recently admitted as more GIs returned home. Lillian always felt reconnected with her art on the nights she taught. She discovered that she was still learning and was coming to understand her techniques and her personal approach to drawing and painting. And nothing gave her more pleasure than to see her students making progress.

Though, as much as she loved teaching, she had to admit that the highlight of her evenings at the hospital was her return home to Charlotte. Even after just a few hours of being apart, there was such joy at their reunion.

"She just woke up," Mrs. Kuntzman said, holding Charlotte in her arms. "As usual, she was an angel." When she handed her to Lillian, the eyes of both mother and daughter broke into unbounded delight.

Mrs. Kuntzman told Lillian how Charlotte had laughed and babbled, almost rolled over all by herself, and was, in general, a most remarkable baby.

"I miss her when it's time to say goodbye." Mrs. Kuntzman now rested her loving eyes on Tommy and Gabriel. "And how are you boys? Did Henry behave himself at the hospital or did he take over the ping pong game like last week?"

Henry and the boys were soon filling her in on the antics of the evening.

Lillian realized how much she enjoyed these brief visits with Mrs. Kuntzman. Especially now that she knew they would be moving. Lately, if she bumped into her in the neighborhood, or returned a baking dish, or just stopped by to say hello, she found herself staying longer, wanting to listen to their old babysitter and friend, filling her eyes with details of her. She felt a sense of loss to know that Charlotte would not experience Mrs. Kuntzman in the same way that Tommy and Gabriel had. Lillian was grateful for her gentle influence on the boys over the years.

Lillian smiled as she rocked back and forth with Charlotte and watched the others laugh at Henry's storytelling. He too had a positive, supportive influence on the boys, and added a sense of merriment to life.

As did Mrs. Wilson, the Kinney family, and all the neighbors. Lillian found herself going to the corner grocery store more often now so that she could chat with the Mancettis and exchange news with the neighbors. They were always so happy to see Charlotte and hear about her latest development.

Lillian told herself that she was being overly sentimental. It wasn't as if they were moving to another state. She could come back and visit anytime she wanted. Charles was so happy about the move. And a new home, a big yard would be –

Charlotte began to fuss and brought Lillian back to the present.

Mrs. Kuntzman was soon at her side. "Ach, no, hungry already my little angel? I fix bottle."

"No, no," laughed Lillian. "I'll feed her at home. Come, boys. It's time we leave. Your father is waiting for us."

"Of course," Mrs. Kuntzman said, rubbing Charlotte's tummy. "Papa looks out the window and says, 'Where's my little bunny?'"

Henry and Tommy, still discussing the patients, brought the baby carriage outside.

"Gabriel, can you carry something?" Mrs. Kuntzman went to the kitchen and returned with a covered plate. "Apple strudel. Is too much for Henry and me," she said. "And you boys enjoy it so."

"So do Mom and Dad," said Gabriel.

"It's true," Lillian said with a laugh. "Charles will be delighted."

That led to a brief conversation about what they were going to bake for the Valentine's Day party the following week, and how they were looking forward to it.

"It's a long time since I celebrate Valentine's Day," said Mrs. Kuntzman.

"Now that you mention it, it's been a long time for me as well. I think we'll enjoy ourselves."

Lillian placed Charlotte in the baby carriage, and they said goodnight to Mrs. Kuntzman and Henry.

Charles had heated up dinner and was setting the table when they arrived. He took Charlotte from Lillian and walked with her around the living room as he told them about a house the real estate agent had told him about.

"With a large and modern kitchen. Though the yard is a little small."

"It sounds wonderful." Lillian opened the oven to check on the casserole, and then looked at her kitchen and smiled. "It's funny how I never really thought about it before. I've always managed to cook anything I wanted in this tiny kitchen." She saw a hint of disappointment in Charles' face and quickly added, "But a big kitchen would be such a pleasure."

He then described a room that could be made into a studio. "With lots of windows and a whole wall that could be built with shelves and cupboards for your supplies."

Lillian smiled as she listened but surprised herself by thinking that the kitchen table had been big enough for all the illustrations she had done over the years. Was she resisting the change? Wasn't it everything she always wanted?

"My own studio! I can finally spread out and organize my materials."

The boys were soon asking about the neighborhood and were excited to hear about a large park nearby with a baseball diamond and a playground with swings for when Charlotte got bigger.

*

The next evening Amy, Mickey and Billy, and Tommy and Gabriel sat around the kitchen table making their signs for the party. They had decided to make them all heart-shaped.

"How about milk and cookies?" Lillian asked them, already pouring out glasses of milk and opening up the cookie tin. "I baked oatmeal raisin cookies today. Gabriel, can you bring these to the table?"

Mickey jumped to his feet. "I'll help."

"Thank you, Mickey." Lillian often noticed how alike Mickey and Tommy were. The older brothers, protective, always helping out. And growing up so quickly, she thought with a pang. The Kinney family had been a big part of their lives here, with Mickey and Billy being the best friends of Tommy and Gabriel.

"We always get good treats here," said Billy, biting into a cookie. "Thanks!"

He had brought his notebook and showed his outline to Lillian.

"Goodness! You've been hard at work. Very impressive." She tried not to smile as she flipped the pages, wondering at the triangle and parallelogram at the end of one list.

"Thankfully, that part's over."

And Billy – always making her laugh. How she would miss them all. And Amy. Sweet, delightful Amy. Lillian noticed that she wore the little locket Tommy had given her at Christmas. She too would be moving over the summer. Lillian looked at the rocking chair Christmas present that all of them had a part in. Such sweet children. Life changes, she told herself. Things never remain the same. She sighed and bit into a cookie.

Amy played with Charlotte and fed her a bottle, cuddling her in the rocking chair. Once she was asleep, Amy placed her in the bassinette, and then she and Lillian began the heart garlands.

The boys cut out hearts of various sizes to be posted on the windows and around the store. They wrote their slogans and information about the raffle on them. They referred to Billy's notes and copied down the suggestions that had been jotted down at the Red String.

Amy got up to take a closer look at Lillian's vintage valentines displayed along the mantel. Out of habit, she slid the little locket back and forth on its chain as she read out a few additional phrases they might be able to use – "To my Queen of Hearts; Sweetheart, think of me this Valentine's Day; To my own true love" – most of which were ignored by the boys.

Tommy made a large heart with the words "Roses are Red, Violets are Blue, Sugar is Sweet, and So are You," thinking that it didn't sound too mushy. "We told Mr. G we'll bring him everything on Saturday and help him decorate the shop."

"And with Valentine's Day next Thursday," said Lillian, "the store will be decorated for several days before." She held up one string of red paper hearts. "We'll have a few of these to give you."

Amy continued working on her strand of hearts and showed them her progress. "I'm making a pink and red garland."

"Mr. G will be happy," said Gabriel. "So many hearts should bring in a lot of people."

As Amy finished her second heart garland, she looked at all the leftover red and pink paper from the hearts they were cutting out. "Look at all these scraps. Gabriel! How about we make little hearts of all sizes, with words if they'll fit, or with a drawing of a rose or something?"

Gabriel's eyes lit up at the vision. "And we can scatter them all over the store! Inside teacups and bowls, on the shelves and in the glass cases."

"And on the table with the cookies and punch," added Amy. "Touches of red and pink all over the store." She was soon cutting out smaller hearts and decorating them.

Lillian looked over at some of the slogans on the larger hearts. She smiled to see the one Gabriel was working on: "We love Mr. G!" and "Red Hearts at the Red String."

Mickey was just finishing up on: "Happy Valentine's Day Mom and Dad."

Tommy held up the heart he was working on and showed it to Amy: "Sweeter than honey, my valentine."

Amy found a pink heart she had made and lifted it for him to read: "I'm sweet on you!"

They laughed at the similar theme. When the others looked up, Tommy slipped his heart under the pile.

"Don't forget, Billy, we still have to make the big sign for the window." Gabriel explained to Lillian, "For the day of the event. We have a big piece of white cardboard but we still have to come up with a slogan."

"Don't worry," said Billy. "We have plenty of words to choose from in my notes. Mr. G won't need it until Thursday."

"If you like, I can decorate the edges with hearts," Lillian offered, "so that it will be ready when you decide on the words."

"That'd help, Mom. It's going to be the main sign, so it needs to look professional."

Billy was busy drawing bows and arrows on all his hearts, along with a few guns. "I hope that Mrs. Jenkins lady doesn't expect us to stay with her niece just because she's our age."

"I think she does," said Gabriel. "She brought her into the shop yesterday and introduced her to me and Mr. G."

"Oh, no," grumbled Billy. "What's she like?"

Gabriel looked up at the ceiling. "It looked like she didn't want to be there. I thought she was going to bust out crying every time I asked her something."

"Oh, no," Billy said again. "We're going to be busy being hosts and getting customers from the street. We won't have time for her. What's her name?"

"Bernice."

"Bernice the niece," groaned Billy. "Maybe we can keep her busy at the punch bowl. Or maybe she can help Mr. G at the counter."

"She's just visiting for a week. Mr. G said we would look after her."

"Oh, no." Billy rolled his eyes and added a rifle, a sling shot, and a volley of arrows to the heart he was working on. Then he spread out the biggest hearts and smiled in approval at his slogans: "A hunter's paradise; Robin Hood loves The Red String Curio Store; All swains welcome to hunt here!"

*

"Hey, Tommy. Are you still awake?"

"Yeah."

"I was just thinking. If we have separate bedrooms in the new house, how will we talk together at night?"

"We can still talk."

"Guess we could visit each other's rooms. Or maybe we'd be out in the treehouse. Maybe we could sleep out there sometimes! That'd be fun." He waited for Tommy's response. "Or we could pitch a tent in the backyard. Like camping."

Gabriel often let his mind roam at night. Sometimes Tommy would respond, sometimes not. Tonight, he freely rambled with his words. He had a feeling Tommy was listening.

"I was thinking… Maybe we could still share a room and let Charlotte have a room to herself."

Gabriel stared up at the ceiling. "She could have her own room since she might want pink curtains or dolls."

"But if it's a big house, we might all get our own rooms," said Tommy.

"Hmm. I didn't think about that." It was Gabriel's turn to be silent now. He folded his arms under his head and gave it some thought. "I guess our rooms would be next to each other. We could make a little cutout in the wall – like a window. You know, by our beds. That way we could still talk."

Tommy gave a groan of exasperation. "People don't do stuff like that, Gabriel."

"I bet Dad would let us. We could even have a little curtain. Say I wanted to read in bed at night, and you didn't. You could just pull the curtain close. But then if you had something to say, or I had a question, we could still talk. What do you think?"

Gabriel waited for Tommy to say something. Maybe he had already fallen asleep. He turned his head to listen. "Hey, Tommy. Do you think I talk too much at night?"

He listened but didn't hear anything. He knew sometimes Tommy got annoyed with him and just wanted to sleep. Sometimes he asked too many questions. Though at other times, it was Tommy who wanted to talk, and he never minded.

Gabriel rolled over on his side. He was still envisioning the little window in the wall with the curtain when Tommy answered.

"No, Gabe. You don't talk too much."

Chapter 11

❧

Mr. Creight was just pulling out of the gas station when he noticed Mrs. Fletcher across the street with a bag of groceries in her arms. The wind fluttered her dark gray coat and white head scarf. He hesitated a moment, and considered driving in the opposite direction. Then he changed his mind and drove up alongside her.

He rolled his window down. "Afternoon, Anne. Can I give you a lift?"

She too hesitated and, out of habit, was about to decline. She glanced up at the scudding clouds against the sharp blue. "Well… Thank you, Abe. It *is* rather cold out." She walked around and climbed into the truck.

They chatted about the weather and the news in town. When they pulled up to her house, Mrs. Fletcher turned to Abe. "May I reciprocate and offer you some dinner?"

He was about to say no, but Mrs. Fletcher added, "Just leftovers, I'm afraid. I made a pot roast dinner yesterday. I still cook too much. Martin had a big appetite."

"I don't want to impose."

"Not at all. You'd be doing me a favor. Save me from eating it all week."

He gave a chuckle.

"Unless you have other plans?"

"Oh, I got plans all right. A cold kitchen and a can of soup."

"That settles it. Come on in. Most of it's in the oven being warmed. Won't take but a minute."

Abe was thinking this was three times at Anne Fletcher's house in the last two weeks. He hoped no one was getting the wrong idea. He knew she wasn't, but you never knew about the neighbors. He also worried that his comment about the soup might give the wrong impression.

"It's not that I don't know how to cook. Jeremy and I had some real feasts. But sometimes, now that it's just me, I don't make the effort."

"I know what you mean. I cook out of habit more than anything."

"I get a solid meal a few times a month when I drive over to my daughters, or one of them comes to visit. They always send leftovers home with me. And Ursula's been bringing things over. So, I get more than enough food. More than I can eat, sometimes."

Mrs. Fletcher didn't buy his overabundance of food. He was just being proud, afraid of appearing needy. She'd play along.

While she heated up a few dishes, she told him that Clem had stopped by earlier. "He's busy with his father and his nephew Donny. And Jessica," she added with a laugh. "But he makes time for me and wants to help me fix up the kitchen." She rubbed her foot along the worn wooden floor. "I'd like to freshen it up. Thought I'd install some of that marbleized linoleum. I do like the look of it."

"I can help Clem. Just let me know when you're ready."

"I will. Thank you, Abe."

That would provide an opportunity to cook up a real meal, she thought. Have Jessica over, as well. She smiled at the thought of cooking for them all. A full table.

She stirred a pan of corn and spoke with her back to Abe. "I saw Jessica and Ursula in town the other day. I feel I better alert you," she said with a glance at him over her shoulder. "Jessica's trying to get me to go to the Valentine's Day dance to help out at the refreshment table. Don't be surprised if they ask you, too."

"They already have. Ursula dropped off some fresh baked bread and told me it would make her happy if I went. But I can't see myself going." He gave a laugh. "When was the last time I was at a dance. Twenty? Thirty years ago?"

"I don't know what Jessica has in mind," said Mrs. Fletcher. She poured the corn into a blue glazed bowl. "Sometimes I think she's just trying to get me to socialize more. Other times…" She shook her head.

"Ursula, too," said Creight. "It bothers her that I'm alone now. We old folks expect it, but I guess when you're young, you think everyone should be part of a couple."

Mrs. Fletcher added a pat of butter to the corn and set the bowl on the table. "But surely, they're not trying to matchmake. At our age."

"You wouldn't think so, but you know how young people are."

"Stars in their eyes. Think pairing up is what the world is all about." She brought the rest of the dishes to the table. "She and Clem are so happy together. I guess that's what's really behind it. I'll let you serve yourself, Abe."

Creight scooted in his chair and looked out at the platter of roast beef and vegetables, the bowls of corn and potatoes. A basket of hot rolls and butter. "This sure beats a can of soup." He filled his plate with a little of everything. Took a bite of the roast and nodded. "Mighty fine, Anne."

"Glad you enjoy it." They ate in companionable silence and then Mrs. Fletcher continued her train of thought. "It's touching, in a way. That they care so much about us. Clem checking up on me."

"Ursula doing the same for me." Creight nodded. "I guess they mean well. I had a falling out with my daughters over the same thing. Always harping at me to get remarried, saying I don't want to be alone all my life. I had to tell them to mind their own business." He buttered a warm roll, dipped it in the juice, and took a bite. "Always pestering me about the widow Havemyer."

Mrs. Fletcher's head snapped up. "Bertha!" She gave it some thought while she also buttered a roll. "I'd say you could do better than that."

Creight chuckled at her remark. "Now. She's a pleasant enough woman. Far as I can tell. Though she talks too much. If I see her coming, I go the other way. Otherwise, I know I'll lose a good hour."

"Martin was the same way. Trying to pair me up with Milton Morsby."

"Milt? And you?" Creight blinked out at the floor trying to imagine Milton with Anne. He shook his head. "I can't see that."

"Neither could I. I don't think I've ever heard him say two words together." Mrs. Fletcher looked at Abe's plate. "Have some more potatoes." She pushed the bowl over to him.

"I've grown fond of Jessica," she continued, "now that I've gotten to know her. I know she'll be good for Clem and that makes me happy. If I go to the dance, it will be for her sake."

"Guess I feel the same about Ursula. She's a sweet girl. Got some heartache up ahead with – you know."

"I know. Her path will not be an easy one." Mrs. Fletcher dished some buttered carrots onto her plate. "I guess it wouldn't hurt us to play along for one night. For their sakes."

Creight jerked his head up. "Go to the Valentine's Day dance? Me? I'd rather muck out the pig sty." He jabbed at his vegetables, and then spoke in a softer tone. "Though I suppose the dance is for the boys who've returned."

Mrs. Fletcher nodded. "That's what I keep telling myself. And if it makes Jessica happy, I'll do it. Man the refreshment table. You could join me. I'd rather have you there than God knows who. It'd make Ursula happy."

"I'd have to stay in the background if I go. Might scare people away."

Mrs. Fletcher laughed at the thought. "Just come for moral support. One hour, and then we can leave. You can help out with getting more ice or forks or whatever."

Creight pinched his eyebrows in thought as he tried to envision himself at the refreshment table. "Guess I could fetch drinks. Haul the garbage away. Just for an hour. Maybe then they'll all back off."

Mrs. Fletcher had to smile at Creight's discomfort. "Shall I tell Jessica we'll go? We'll smile and nod, and eat heart-shaped cookies and say how delicious they are."

"Fetch ice, haul garbage. And that would be that."

Mrs. Fletcher gave a curt nod to their limited, but polite, involvement. "We'll be cordial. And smile when Jessica stops by the table. Though we don't want to encourage her matchmaking. She doesn't have the knack for it."

"I'll say. It could go to her head. She might try her hand with Bertha."

Mrs. Fletcher let out a laugh. "And Milton!"

Creight also allowed himself to laugh. "Now that would be a pair!" They chuckled at the image of the unlikely couple as Mrs. Fletcher cleared the dishes. She cut a few slices of coffee cake and made a fresh pot of coffee.

"I'm afraid I can't take credit for this," she said, handing a slice to Abe. "I bought it at the bakery today. I don't bake like I used to." She gave a soft smile. "Martin had such a sweet tooth."

As the evening drew on, they grew more comfortable with each other, now that the obstacle of matchmaking had been addressed, resolved, and dismissed. Now that it was out of the way, they could just enjoy each other's company.

Mostly they talked of their lost sons, the shock of receiving the telegrams, the memories. Creight talked about the drive for clothing over Christmas, and how hard it was to pack up Jeremy's things. "Yet it was the right thing to do. Ursula was there. Her kindness helped me to get through that day."

"I've been putting it off. There's another drive coming up. I know I should just do it, gather up Martin's clothes. Life goes on." She looked towards his bedroom, as if seeing him. "Martin would want me to. I know it. I suppose they're still here with us, aren't they?"

"It'd be a mistake to think they're gone. I know Jeremy would want me to go on. To be tough like I taught him to be." He took a sip of coffee. "Not sure I ever really succeeded. He had a gentle nature. Like his mother."

"Like you too, Abe. Beneath that crusty exterior." She gave a tender smile at his rough farmer's hand holding her delicate gold-rimmed cup.

They finished their coffee and Mrs. Fletcher took their dishes to the kitchen counter.

As Abe put on his jacket, Mrs. Fletcher stood with her hands before her. "You've helped me to decide my mind. I'll go through Martin's things for the drive. If you can do it, so can I. I dare say I'm as strong as you are."

Abe smiled at the understatement, but kept it to himself, and said his goodnight.

Chapter 12

෴

"It's hard not to worry when I don't know what he's up to." Lillian tried to keep calm, but part of her remained troubled at Gabriel's unpredictability. "He was supposed to go straight to the hospital with Tommy after school. I knew I shouldn't have allowed him to go without me."

"I'm sure there's a simple explanation," said Charles. "We've gone through this before with Gabriel."

"Countless times! Worrying me to death. All I ask is that he's honest with me."

Charles wrapped his arms around her. "We don't know that he wasn't honest. Give him a chance to explain." He pulled her onto the couch where they could watch Charlotte as she slept peacefully in her bassinette.

"You're right. I know he wouldn't do anything intentionally wrong. But why was he wandering around Macy's all on his own? He's eleven. I wouldn't even want Tommy doing that."

Charles placed his hand on Lillian's arm and gave a hushed laugh. "Look." He pointed towards the bassinette. Charlotte gave a little twitch and one side of her mouth turned up in a smile.

"Oh, how sweet! Do you think she's dreaming?" That little half smile eased Lillian's mind.

They sat in quiet comfort gazing at Charlotte, their fingers entwined.

"Any word from Izzy?"

"No. I was hoping to hear from her by now. She'll have to make a decision soon. I wish they'd both come back here and figure things out. I really can't stand not knowing what's going on. I hope so badly..."

"I know. I'm sure the love is there, on both sides. But those were difficult years for them. We've been able to pick up where we left off."

"It must be so different for them, over there." Lillian briefly tried to imagine what their lives in London might look like. "You've been home for a month and a half, but sometimes I'm afraid I'm just dreaming. It still feels like a miracle that you're here."

He gave a smile. "If it wasn't for Red, who knows – I might still be in England, waiting for transport home. I can never repay him."

Lillian curled closer to him. "We're so lucky, Charles. I never take it for granted. My life is perfect now and I don't need anything else."

Charles gave her a playful squeeze. "But you would like a studio, wouldn't you? And a bigger kitchen. And more room for the kids."

"Well, yes. The boys have outgrown their tiny room. Tommy's feet already hang over the end of his bed. And Charlotte's going to need a playpen soon. But honestly, *this* – you in my arms, Charlotte before us, the boys home soon – this is happiness."

The boys soon arrived home, abuzz with news from the Red String.

"The shop looks really good," said Tommy. "The heart garlands you and Amy made are hanging in the windows and by the front counter. And Gabriel and Billy found lots of stuff and it's all spread out on tables in the front."

"We had to set up two more tables," said Gabriel. "And there are hearts everywhere! I didn't know we made so many."

"Junior copied out at least ten poems, maybe more, and Mr. G put them in frames. And he's going to make some more."

"All day long, customers said how cheerful the shop looked and that they'd be sure to stop by for –" Gabriel sniffed the air and his eyes widened. "Baked ziti?"

Lillian smiled. "Yes. Go wash up and then we'll eat. There's something I want to ask you about."

When they were all seated, and after Gabriel and Tommy had recounted their day at the Red String with Amy and Mickey and Billy, Lillian turned to Gabriel.

"I ran into Mrs. Connor at the grocery store. She said she saw you at Macy's. That you passed her several times."

Gabriel nodded as he chewed. "I did. I must have said hi to her five times." He saw that Lillian was waiting for more. "I was polite." He took another bite of pasta. "This is really good, Mom."

Lillian set her fork down. "Gabriel. You were at Macys, wandering around alone? When I thought you were with Tommy and Henry at the hospital?" She looked over at Tommy. "Did you know anything about this?"

"I told Tommy I was going there. He knew where I was." He looked to Charles and Tommy, and back to Lillian. "I wasn't hiding anything."

"What on earth were you doing there? Why weren't you at the hospital?"

"I went there afterwards."

"But – what were you doing!"

"Oh! I was looking for someone. It's a big store. It took me a while."

Lillian looked over at Charles at the unexpected answer, her cheeks growing pink in exasperation.

Charles helped himself to more ziti and suppressed a smile. "Why don't you tell us about it, Gabriel?"

"Well, it's kind of a long story. It has to do with Matty."

"The patient at the hospital?" asked Charles.

Gabriel nodded. "He's going to come to the party. The Valentine's Day party at the Red String."

"What –" Lillian began to ask, but Charles made a small gesture for her to allow Gabriel to continue.

Tommy jumped in to help the story along. "You remember his fiancée? Well, Gabriel was thinking that it would be nice for her to come to the party, too."

Lillian was growing more confused. "I thought they were no longer engaged."

Gabriel picked up the thread. "Matty yelled at her and told her not to come back. But I don't think he really meant it. Anyway, I wanted to invite her to the party but all I knew was that her name was Carol and that she worked at Macy's. So, I went there to look for her."

Charles exchanged a smile with Lillian. "Did you find her?"

Gabriel nodded. "She was happy to see me and said she's going to come. She's really nice."

Lillian let out a deep breath and began to eat, going over Gabriel's story. "Do they know the other will be there?"

"I told her that Matty was coming," said Gabriel.

Was he trying to get them back together? Lillian wondered. "But – what makes you think it's a good idea?"

Gabriel twisted his mouth as he tried to explain his idea. "Well, I thought if they could see each other outside of the hospital, then he wouldn't be a patient anymore and she wouldn't be a visitor. They would just be normal people." He bit into a breadstick and nodded, as if he had summed it up clearly. "Besides, the Red String makes people happy. I thought they might have a good time."

Lillian looked out in bewilderment. She never knew if Gabriel was just the happy-go-lucky boy he was on the surface, or if there were deeper impulses that ran in him, guiding him through the intricacies of human nature. It was impossible to know.

"I think your idea was a good one, Gabriel," Charles said. "But you worry us when we don't know where you are. Next time, tell us. Or take Tommy with you."

Gabriel gave it a second's consideration and smiled. "Okay."

"Sorry," said Tommy. "I should have thought of that when he told me where he was going."

"Yeah, me too." Gabriel leaned forward to see how much ziti was left, and when Lillian nodded at him, he took another helping. "I think we're going to have a lot of food for the party. Henry said Mrs. Kuntzman is going to bake cookies and treats and some kind of a Valentine's Day cake. He's helping her."

"I'll be sure to bring her some of Annette's honey and maple syrup." Lillian smiled at Charles, happy to move on to the subject of the party. "And Mrs. Wilson and I are going to bake cookies. So, there should be enough to go around."

"Mickey said his mom is, too," said Tommy.

"It sounds like the party will be a great success," said Charles.

"We sure hope so," said Gabriel. "I think it will be a yearly event. Mr. G said next year we'll —" Gabriel stopped when he remembered that he probably wouldn't be there next year. "Is there any more chocolate pie left?"

*

Later that evening, Charles was stretched out on the couch with Charlotte asleep in his arms. The boys had played with her after dinner, and then Lillian had given her a bath. While the boys did their homework at the table, Charles sat in the rocking chair smiling down at Charlotte as he fed her a bottle. Then he walked with her for a bit, and lay on the couch, cradling her close to him.

Lillian had draped the afghan over him and returned to the kitchen table.

Charles woke to hear them speaking in low voices, as if not wanting to wake him or Charlotte. It sounded like a continuation of Mr. G's plans for next year.

"Will you be sorry not to be working at the Red String, Gabriel?" Lillian asked.

"Maybe I can find a way to still work there. Ride my bike in or something."

Tommy looked up from his homework. "I told him it would be too far for that."

"What about you, Tommy? How do you feel about moving?"

"Amy's already leaving. Moving away. I guess you just have to get used to things."

Lillian looked carefully at him. "And I know you're sad about that. Do you think this is too much change in one year?"

"I'll get used to it, Mom. Remember how I didn't want to move from Brooklyn?"

Lillian gave a laugh. "You were furious. You didn't want to leave your friends."

"But then I got to like it here."

They were quiet for a few moments. Then Lillian shifted in her chair. "The move into Manhattan was good for us. I'm sure the next one will be too."

Tommy nodded but his voice filled with disappointment. "I'll have to give up my job at Mancetti's. And I'll miss my friends. And the neighborhood."

"Me too," said Gabriel. "There won't be anything like The Red String Curio Store. Anywhere in the world. Not with Mr. G and Junior and Dusty. Henry. And Mrs. Kuntzman! She'll miss out on Charlotte growing up. I don't think she'll be happy about that."

"I guess we'll all get used to it," said Tommy. "Like Amy's going to have to. What about you, Mom?"

"I certainly love the idea of a bigger home. Your father has put so much into researching neighborhoods and looking at houses. It's all very exciting. And you boys are getting way too big for your bedroom. Where will Charlotte sleep when she gets older?"

"But – how do you feel about leaving our neighborhood?" asked Gabriel.

Tommy watched closely for how she would respond. "Will you miss it? And being close to your job?"

"I'm lucky. With the arrangement I have with the publishing house, I can work from anywhere. And it would be a dream come true to have a real studio."

Again, there was a long silence. "Of course, I love our neighborhood and will miss it. And our neighbors. There are a lot of good memories in this place. I've loved being close to Central Park, and having so much of the city within walking distance. But it will be a tradeoff. We'll have a big yard. We can grow our own vegetables. I can even have a flower garden."

Gabriel nodded and gave a faint smile.

"We're not complaining, Mom," Tommy said. "We'll be happy about it. Like you and Dad are."

"Well, it's getting late." Her voice filled with forced enthusiasm. "Finish your homework and then go wash up. You can read for a bit."

Chapter 13

∾

On Sunday, Jessica had lunch with Clem and his father and Donny. Afterwards, she and Clem decided to stop by Mrs. Fletcher's house and bring her a slice of the apple pie she had baked.

Mrs. Fletcher answered the door with her long hair still damp and a bath towel in her hand. "Oh, you caught me with my hair down. Come on in. Have a seat. I'll just pin it up and be right back. Clem, turn the kettle on, will you? I'll fix us some coffee."

Jessica looked at the older woman in surprise. She looked completely different with her hair down. Not at all stern, and to Jessica's amazement, quite beautiful. She wondered why she had never noticed it before.

"Mrs. Fletcher!" Jessica observed her more closely. "I never knew you had such lovely hair."

She let out a laugh. "Now you're going too far, Jessica. My hair is mostly gray now."

"No, it's still mostly dark, and there's a beautiful wave to it. You should wear it down."

"It's too long for that." Mrs. Fletcher returned the towel to the bathroom and came back with a few hairpins. She twisted her hair, wound it into a coil, and pinned it in place. Stern again, prim, no nonsense. "I've worn it this way for the last – must be thirty years."

"Oh, what a waste! Have you ever thought of cutting it? Say, to the shoulder. That way you could leave it down." Jessica tried to think of a practical reason to bolster her argument. "Just think how quickly it would dry."

"You sound just like Martin. He was always telling me to cut my hair. This style suits me fine."

When they had made the coffee and were seated, Mrs. Fletcher placed her hands on the table. "Now, Jessica, you'll be pleased to know that I *will* help out at the refreshment table at the dance. For the first hour, and no more. And I've managed to corral Abe Creight into joining me, though it took some doing."

Jessica's face lit up and she flashed a smile to Clem. "Oh, I'm so happy! Thank you, Mrs. Fletcher. Wait until I tell Ursula."

"We want to do our part for the returning servicemen. It's nothing more than that." She looked pointedly at Jessica. "You understand?"

"Of course. Clem, did you hear? Mrs. Fletcher is going to help us with refreshments. So, I've got all three hours covered."

Mrs. Fletcher caught the wink Jessica gave to Clem. *Oh, let her have her fun,* she thought. "I hope the refreshment committee will be happy."

"The – oh, yes. The committee. They'll be hugely relieved. Thank you."

Clem had to smile at Jessica's happiness. "Do you want us to stop by for you?"

Mrs. Fletcher shook her head. "You two will be busy. I'll catch a ride with Abe."

Rather than see another 'I told you so' smile of triumph from Jessica, Clem looked around and saw several empty boxes set out. "What are the boxes for?"

"There's another clothing drive for refugees next week. I thought I'd see what I can round up."

Clem took a sip of coffee. "Dad and I are doing the same thing. Donny's getting so tall. He's outgrown some of his clothes. I can take whatever boxes you have along with ours."

"I'd appreciate that."

They were soon talking about local news, the number of boys from town still in the process of returning, and how this winter wasn't as cold as feared. Clem leaned back in his chair. "Anything I can help you with while I'm here?"

"Thank you, Clem, but no. I can take care of most things. Abe stopped by to fix my back door. I think someone dropped him a hint that I needed help."

Jessica brushed at a thread on her sweater.

"It was kind of him to help out an old class-mate. And I was able to get him to eat a solid meal. I *will* need your help once the linoleum comes in. Abe offered to help you with it."

Clem nodded and finished his coffee. "And Donny will give us a hand. We'll have it done in no time."

When they left, Jessica tugged on Clem's arm, as if expecting a comment on her victory.

"Well?"

Clem had to smile. "Abe fixed her door. She fed him. Is that what you wanted?"

"It's a start. And they're going to help out at the dance."

"Because you pressured them into it."

"Now you sound like Jimmy," Jessica said.

Clem slipped his arm through hers and gave her a squeeze. "Truth is, Jessica, no one can say no to you and your charms. Least of all me."

Jessica laughed and kissed his cheek.

*

Once in a great while, and only if she could reciprocate, Mrs. Fletcher accepted help when it was offered. Especially from Clem and sometimes Donny, since they lived so close by. However, later that evening, Mrs. Fletcher did something she rarely did. She asked for help.

"I'm so sorry to bother you, Abe. Come in. Have you had dinner? Can I get you a cup of coffee?"

"I've eaten. Everything all right?" He fixed his eyes on her, concerned.

"Yes. It's just – I was…" Her eyes darted around as she sought words to explain why she had called him.

He saw her struggle and placed a hand on her shoulder. "What is it?"

"I was going through Martin's things. For the clothing drive. Clem's going to drop them off for me."

Abe noticed three open boxes filled with clothes.

A slight tremble entered her voice. "I packed them up, and I – I… I had a hard time. Loner that I am, I don't think I can do it alone."

"I can help."

She raised her face to Abe and he saw a vulnerability there that surprised him. The same weakness and desperation that had filled him when he was trying to round up Jeremy's clothes.

Mrs. Fletcher tried to wave away her concern. "I know I'm being foolish. I want Martin's clothes to keep someone warm over there. Some boy his own age. I want that. I do. I packed up his boots and winter coat, his pants and shirts. I was fine. And –" She brought her hand to her mouth and tried to steel herself.

Abe put an arm around her.

"And then I folded one of his favorite shirts. His blue plaid flannel. It made me see him again. Right there. Laughing, smiling, calling me 'Mom.' My baby. My baby boy. And I –"

Abe held her in his arms and patted her back as she broke down. "I know. I know. I went through the same thing. No one tells you how hard it's going to be."

She buried her face in his chest and sobbed, her whole body shaking. He comforted her as best he could – stiffly at first – then gently, holding her, saying *there, there*, and stroking her back. "I've broken down more times than I care to count. Can't help myself. There's no balm for that gaping hole. I'm so sorry, Anne."

As she released deep, heart-wrenching sobs, Abe's eyes teared up. That kind of pain was bottomless. There was no way it was going to lessen.

She kept her head on his chest and struggled to speak. "Sometimes I think I can't go on. I try. I think I'm all right – and then..."

"I know. I know how it is." He reached into his pocket and gave her his hankie. "It's clean."

She gave a small laugh. "Thank you, Abe." She dried her eyes and blew her nose. "I'll launder it, of course."

Now it was his turn to smile at this most practical of women.

"I'm ashamed to admit it. But I couldn't bear to be alone tonight. I felt so –" She raised her face to him again. "I didn't know who else to call. Who wouldn't think me just a pitiful old woman."

"Now, now, no one would think such a thing. There's a lot of loss these past years, a lot of pain. It's a hard time for many folks." He patted her back again. "Of course, you did right to call me."

"I knew you would understand."

Her tears slowly lessened, followed by a few deep sighs. "It was handling his things that did it, that brought everything back. The clothes I ironed and mended for him all these years. And then boxing them away. It was like I lost him all over again.

And I – I didn't want to be alone with it." She pressed the hankie to her eyes. "Thank you for being here."

"You call me anytime you need me. I know what it feels like. I can come anytime."

"Just to know that. Makes me feel not quite so – desperate."

They stood in silence and she used the handkerchief to dry her face. "I'll do the same for you. You come to me if there are difficult times."

He nodded.

"I mean it, Abe. If you don't promise me, then I won't call you. It has to work both ways. Don't you go trying to be all tough and stoic."

"All right. I promise. It'll be a first for me. But I promise."

She let out a final sigh and put her head in her hands. Then she took a deep, jagged breath. "Let me wash my face. Will you stay and join me in a glass of port?"

He nodded. "I'll fold the boxes shut and stack them by the door." He watched her leave and tended to the boxes. Afterwards, he sat on the edge of the couch, wishing there was more he could do to help her.

In a few minutes she returned. She stopped to squeeze his shoulder in gratitude, and then went to the kitchen. She carried in the bottle of port and two small glasses, filled them, and sat next to him on the couch.

After a few moments of silence, and few calming sips of port, they began to speak about their lives, and dealing with the loss of their sons. That led to talking about their marriages, the loneliness they felt after their spouses died, and the many ways they combated it over the years – mostly with work and keeping busy. And finally, they spoke of their newfound friendship.

"Jessica and Clem stopped by for a visit today. They offered to pick me up for the dance. When I told them you were going to take me, they broke into smiles. I told them we would do our duty and serve at the table. It made them both so happy. I think we made the right decision, Abe."

Creight took a sip and nodded. "If it makes the young people happy."

"It won't hurt us to play along for an hour. At our age it doesn't much matter."

"Most certainly not," Abe agreed.

Mrs. Fletcher refilled their glasses and smiled as she remembered the wink Jessica gave to Clem at her ruse. "They looked so pleased with themselves. I suppose we should be flattered."

"Or at least amused. At our age?"

They both gave a light chuckle.

"That's youth," Mrs. Fletcher said. "Always with their heads in the clouds. But you know, I think Martin would be happy."

Creight stared out and nodded. "Jeremy would be, too. Funny to think of doing something for them, after they're gone."

"I was thinking the same thing."

He took the last sip of his port, gave her a small nod, and placed his hands on his knees, preparing to leave.

Mrs. Fletcher patted his arm. "I'll be all right now, Abe. I can't tell you how grateful I am to you. You saved me from a terrible night."

They rose to their feet, but when he heard her words, he stared hard at her.

"What is it?" she asked.

"Nothing. It's just —" He looked away, and then held her gaze. "I never thought I'd be of any use to anyone again."

"Oh, Abe." She gave him a hug. "You have a world of kindness in you that warms my frigid heart."

He gave a soft smile and put his hand on her cheek. "Not frigid. Lovely." He kissed her lips. Then pulled back in surprise. "I'm sorry. I don't know where that came from."

She drew him to her. "That's the nicest thing that has happened to me in a long time."

They wrapped their arms around each other and kissed again, and for the first time in a long time, they were not so alone in the world.

Chapter 14

෨

Another week had passed, and still Izzy waited for Red to speak about their future. Surely after the time they had spent together, he knew that she couldn't live without him. There could be no doubt.

She believed he felt the same. She knew he did. But then why hadn't he spoken about it? The previous day she had hinted at marrying, jokingly saying, "If we were married, at least we could live together. My room is like a closet. I think it is a closet." She waited for Red to respond, but he had only smiled and looked away.

How long was she prepared to wait?

Not a day longer, was the answer she gave herself. They were going to meet in the late afternoon for a walk and dinner. She would force him to speak about their future.

Bundled up in their coats and scarves and gloves, they strolled through the village and along the path by the stream.

"How was your day at the orphanage?" he asked.

"I'm growing attached to the children. Yet it's such happiness when some of them are claimed by relatives or reunited with a parent believed to be dead. Still, there are so many." She was overwhelmed by the need for everything. Food, clothing, love, hope, healing. Like Red had told her, the need was endless here and would remain so for a long time.

But they didn't have an endless amount of time. They were not getting younger. And she was not prepared to give up her job. At least, not yet.

They ambled along the stream, stopping to watch the sun as it began to set over the little stone bridge.

"Red..."

He turned a worried face to her. Anytime she began to bring up the subject, a look of anxiety filled his eyes.

"I have to think about going back home."

"I know. I know you do, Izzy. I've... I've been wanting to speak to you about that. I don't think you should give up your job." He broke off, and they resumed walking.

Her heart began to sink. Wasn't he going to put up a fight for her? Surely, he was not going to reject her now? Not after their time together and the closeness they were rebuilding.

He rubbed his eyes and looked up at the sky. "Much as I love it here, the sense of purpose I have... I have to think about getting back, too. There are others to fill my place now. And my family wants me to come home, of course. I could finish my degree on the Servicemen's Readjustment Act. What they're calling the GI Bill. I could work and make a life for myself."

He faced her, as if he was about to say more – and then turned away.

Izzy could almost hear his thoughts. He couldn't bring himself to ask her to join her life with his – a second time. He felt he had forfeited that right.

They walked in silence, deep in their thoughts. Then Izzy smiled and linked her arm with Red's.

"I've thought so many times about the night we met. We began with a dance."

Red gave a soft laugh. "We began with an argument."

Izzy also laughed at the memory. "No – by that time I was already hopelessly in love with you. I was just angry about it. Angry that you didn't have to do much to claim my heart."

"I felt the same. I was afraid of you – of your power over me."

Izzy gave a laugh of disbelief. "So, we were both fighting our love."

"Well, it didn't last long, as I remember."

"No, it melted away as soon as you asked me to dance." She playfully stood before him and raised her face to him. "Come, dance with me." She took his hand and placed it on her waist.

Red smiled. "I don't hear any music, Izzy."

"I do. You're just not listening." She took his other hand and began to move.

Red began to hum the words to 'With Time on My Hands.' "You remember?"

"I'll never forget. That became our song."

He stopped. "Izzy. I know it's only been a short while since you came here. But we're happy, aren't we?" He searched her face for the answer he wanted.

"Yes, we're happy. I'm almost desperately happy – but not quite."

When he rubbed at his eyes again, Izzy pulled his hand down. "No, Red. Look at me. Don't look back, don't look away. Look at us. What do you want?"

He held her face in his hands. "You know what I want, Izzy."

"Then what are we waiting for?"

"I'm afraid of – of hoping for happiness that I don't deserve."

"Red, when you answered my letter asking if you still loved me, that was all I needed to hear."

"I meant it, Izzy. I have loved only you." He took her hands and pressed them to his heart.

"And you said you wished the best for me. You *are* the best for me, Red."

"Then – then – will you…"

Izzy threw her arms around him. "Of course, I'll marry you."

Chapter 15

❧

On the evening of the Valentine's Day Dance, Creight stopped by Mrs. Fletcher's home to drive her and the cookies she had baked to the hall.

He was glad he had left his suit out after last month's double wedding. It no longer carried the faint scent of mothballs. Two events in one year and it was only February. He wasn't sure how he felt about that.

This event should last as long as the wedding reception had. An hour. In and out. Then home. Unless Anne wanted to stay longer, of course. It gave him a new sense of purpose to think that he had helped her out. Strange how much could change in a month. They had not seen eye to eye at the wedding. And now – Well, no need to get ahead of himself.

He knocked on her door, mildly embarrassed by the small box of chocolates in his hand. He had purchased it on impulse that afternoon when he saw it at the counter of the grocery store. The display read: "Candy's Dandy. Keep it Handy." He read it twice and decided that it didn't sound too romantic, despite the box being heart-shaped. Now he doubted his choice. He didn't want her to think –

The door opened and all thoughts of embarrassment and dandy candy vanished. His jaw dropped. There stood Anne – but a younger, happier version of herself. He could scarce believe it was the same woman.

"Come in, Abe. Oh, chocolates! Thank you. I'll save these for later. Well, don't gawk at me. What do you think?" She put a hand to her hair. It was parted on the side, hanging in loose waves to her shoulders. "Was I wrong to cut it?"

He stepped inside and continued to stare at her. She wore a rose and gray floral dress that hugged her figure, and a bit of lipstick if he wasn't mistaken. She was breathtaking. But he couldn't say that.

He ran his hand over her hair and she smiled up at him.

"Looks nice, Anne. You look real nice." He felt weak in the knees. What was wrong with him?

"I'm still not used to it. I catch my reflection in the mirror and do a double take."

"It suits you. I can't say how, but it does."

She slipped into her coat and lifted the box of cookies. "I hope people don't think I'm trying to catch you. You know how people talk."

"We don't have to worry about what other people think. One of the perks of getting older. Though you don't seem to fit in that category anymore."

"Oh, Abe," she laughed. "I feel every bit as old as my gray hair indicates. Though – I do feel lighter. Happier, if that makes any sense."

He tried not to keep snatching glances at her as he drove them to the hall. Yet he couldn't get over the transformation. He wanted to reach over and caress the silky waves. See her smile again at his touch. He kept his eyes on the road and told himself he was an old fool.

When they entered the hall and hung up their coats, they heard a commotion behind them, and Jessica ran up.

Dressed in her pale pink dress and beaming in delight, she impulsively hugged Mrs. Fletcher. "You did it! Oh, it looks wonderful. Clem, look!"

A few other women walked up and commented on her hair. Mrs. Fletcher simply replied, "It was Jessica's idea. And I thought she was right. Time for a change."

Jessica noticed that Creight looked uncomfortable, hanging back with the box of cookies in his hands.

"This way, Mr. Creight," she said. "Clem, show them where the refreshment table is. I'll let the committee know that our first shift has arrived."

While Clem showed them to the back of the hall, Jessica ran to tell Shirley and Sue Ellen about Mrs. Creight's hair and how it had been all her idea. She loved it when people actually took her advice.

Within a half hour, the hall became a crowded scene of greetings and laughter, handshakes and embraces. The band tuned up and started to play and the tables filled up with couples and families and friends.

Eugene and Edna had returned the day before and rode in with Jimmy and Gladys. Paul drove Kate, Ursula and Frankie. They were running somewhat behind schedule because Ursula had received a letter from Friedrich and was beside herself with joy. The word was that he wouldn't ship out until sometime in March. She was distracted by happiness the entire day, picking up Frankie and kissing him, deciding to make another batch of sugar cookies, and disappearing to a quiet space to read the letter again and again. It meant that Friedrich was safe. He was still being well fed. Though apart, they were still in the same country. She considered the well-timed letter her own private Valentine's Day gift from Friedrich.

Paul found them all a table next to the others. Jimmy and Eugene were drinking beers, laughing and talking with friends who stopped by the table. Edna was introduced to more people than she could keep track of.

"Everyone is so warm and welcoming to me," she told Eugene. "This feels like home already."

Eugene threw his arm around her shoulder and whispered into her ear. "That's because everyone who meets you falls in love with you. As I did."

Ed and Opal sat at an adjacent table and Ursula was soon sharing the news of Friedrich with Ed.

Paul looked around nervously, not wanting to see Lucille on the arm of someone else. He was still kicking himself for avoiding her.

When Jessica and Clem came over with drinks and a plate of cookies, Kate and Ursula remarked on the transformation of Mrs. Fletcher. Jessica explained how it had all started with her and Clem dropping by for a visit.

"Gladys," said Jessica, "go take a look at the pies and cakes. Take Edna while there's still so much to choose from." She bit into a cookie. "Oh Jimmy," she said in a teasing tone, "did you see who was at the refreshment table?"

"Yes, I did. On my way to the bar. And Creight looks his usual cantankerous self. Only here because you two pestered him into it." He unfairly included Ursula, only because he hated to admit that he might be wrong.

"That he's here at all shocks the heck out of me," said Eugene.

"I'm surprised, too," said Ursula. She looked over at Mr. Creight and Mrs. Fletcher, standing side by side, serving drinks, handing out plates, talking with people. She was struck by how handsome they looked together. It was more than his suit and her new hairstyle. "They look… Somehow, they look right together, don't they? Or at least comfortable with each other. Do you think –"

"Let's just see what happens," said Jessica. "I saw Lucille, Paul, and does she ever look beautiful. She's wearing the most gorgeous purple dress. She's an absolute vision!"

"Who –" Paul caught himself. It wasn't his business who she was with. He'd have to try to repair the damage. Call her. At least tell her, explain that – He groaned to think that he was still tongue-tied when it came to her. Even in his head. What chance did he have? He didn't want to look in the direction Jessica pointed to. He didn't think he could stand it if she looked like she was in love with someone else. He gave himself another mental kick.

Several girls walked slowly past Paul, and two or three stopped to say hello. But he wasn't his usual gregarious self. He exchanged a few words with them, picked at the label on his beer bottle, and tried not to look out at the crowd.

Kate turned to him. "Aren't you going to ask anyone to dance? What's wrong with you? This is just the kind of thing you love."

"How about you, Mom. Care to dance?"

So, Paul danced with Kate, and then politely asked a few friends. Then he danced with Opal while Ed and Ursula took a spin. When he sat down, he declared that he didn't feel like dancing any more. He took Frankie on his lap and talked with him while he fed him some cake.

But when he looked up, there was the vision, standing before him. Radiant, beautiful, raven-haired, her lively brown eyes smiling down at him.

He couldn't get any words out.

Lucille leaned over. "Hello, Frankie. Is that cake good? I was hoping your uncle might ask me to dance."

Clem reached over and took Frankie, bouncing him on his lap.

"Hi, Lucille," said Jessica. "Paul was just saying how beautiful you look tonight and that he was going to ask you to dance. And here you are!"

Paul stood and would have given Jessica a scowl, but he was looking around for Lucille's date to scowl at. He stepped aside from the table to speak to Lucille in private.

"Where's your date?" he asked in a challenging manner, wondering if she had just stopped by to torment him.

"I don't have a date."

"He canceled?" Paul almost shouted at the indignity. He'd like to give the guy a good punch in the nose.

"I never had a date. I came alone." She raised her eyebrows. "Are we going to dance or not?"

He walked with her to the dance floor, replaying the afternoon when he saw her in town. "But when I invited you to come with me, you said you were already going."

She nodded. "Jessica said you were planning to go alone. I thought if you can, then so can I. I have to say I'm enjoying being on my own. The freedom is nice. Not being tied down to any one partner. Jessica said you called that – playing the field?"

Paul blushed at his words and realized how full of himself it made him sound.

"I – that's not what I was doing. I was going to ask you – you know…" Now that Lucille was in his arms, and they were moving to the music, it was easier to let his heart do the talking for him. "I think you know how I feel about you, Lucille."

"I thought I did. But I was beginning to think I was mistaken. That all those letters meant nothing to you."

He held her closer and looked into her eyes. "Those letters are what got me through the hard times. Your words. Your advice. And your, your..."

"My love for you? Because I meant it, Paul. I wasn't just saying that because you were a soldier far from home."

And so began the continuation of the thread that had begun in their letters. They danced and talked and didn't change partners for the entire evening.

When the band took a break, Jimmy and Gladys returned from the dance floor, fanning themselves, and joined the others. Jimmy shook his head at Paul who had walked outside for a breath of air with Lucille.

"I told him he was a goner. I knew he was stuck on her. I'm right about most things, Jess." He took a swig of beer and pointed the bottle to the refreshment table. "Creight and Mrs. Fletcher serving cake? That doesn't count."

Eugene gave a laugh. "Take a good look, because it's the last time we'll ever see them together."

"At any rate, I hope your matchmaking has come to a close," said Jimmy.

Jessica answered with a smile. "I believe it has."

Ed stood with Opal and announced, "Well, this is our shift. One hour and then it's back to the dance floor."

"I'll go with you," said Kate. "Eugene and Jimmy, come help me carry a few drinks back for everyone."

"I'll come too," said Jessica. "I fancy a glass of lemonade."

Ursula smiled at Jessica, knowing that she wanted to gloat a bit in front of Jimmy and Eugene.

For Creight's part, the dreaded one hour was over. It had turned out to be rather enjoyable. He and Anne had served cake and pie and cookies. He had gone for more ice and put out new treats. They had spoken together when they could, and were both glad that they had come. And they were now glad that it was over.

The plan was to leave after their shift. Call it a day. Duty fulfilled.

Ed and Opal traded places with them and exchanged a few words, while Kate decided on which drinks to get.

Though they wouldn't admit it to Jessica, Jimmy and Eugene were in a state of disbelief at seeing Abe Creight at the dance at all, let alone helping out at the refreshment table, let alone chatting with the stern Mrs. Fletcher – who looked anything but stern tonight. She was positively glowing. And Abe looked a good deal younger himself. But an hour handing out treats to returning servicemen was all it was, whatever Jessica might think. Show over. Creight and Mrs. Fletcher could now go back to being proud, stubborn, and difficult.

However, what happened next shattered all such expectations – though it was prompted by nothing more remarkable than the appearance at the refreshment table of Bertha Havemyer on the arm of Milton Morsby.

"Oooh, let's see," said the amiable Bertha, fluttering her fingers. She pointed out various items to Milt. "This looks like date bread, and I do believe it was made by Ethel Homer, which guarantees it will be delicious. Hello, Abe! Anne Fletcher, how nice to see you! And we can't pass up this apple pie. We'll take a slice of that, please. And these," she said, pointing to a plate of sugar cookies, "I made myself, so we must have a few of those..."

When Creight and Mrs. Fletcher beheld the most unlikely of couples standing before them, they lowered their heads and busied themselves with plates and napkins. A close-lipped laugh escaped Abe and Mrs. Fletcher's hand flew to her mouth, though she was less successful at hiding her amusement.

Jimmy and Eugene traded looks. What was going on?

Creight and Mrs. Fletcher might have kept their composure, but when Bertha continued to pile up the treats, describing them in detail to the silent Milt, another stifled laugh escaped them and their shoulders began to shake.

Then, they couldn't resist doing the one thing guaranteed to make them lose all control – they looked at each other.

Ed and Opal – greatly amused, and less surprised than the others at the rapport between Abe Creight and Anne Fletcher – covered for them as they stepped away from the table and gave in to their laughter. It grew and grew until Anne Fletcher put her head on Abe's chest and he leaned over in mirth, placing his hand familiarly on her back. With all eyes on them, and Bertha merrily stacking up desserts for Milt, Abe took Anne's hand.

"Our only escape is to take to the dance floor," he said, leading her away.

They laughed freely once they were safely dancing, which covered any discomfort in the fact that neither had danced in long years.

Jessica linked her hands behind her back and gave Jimmy a big smile.

"Dang. I need a drink," he said.

Eugene, who thought he knew Abe Creight better than anyone, added, "I must be seeing things." They went to the bar together, while Ed and Opal served drinks for Kate and Jessica to take back to the others.

More friends and neighbors stopped by to visit their table, and when Paul and Lucille returned to the dance floor, the difference in them was unmistakable. They were no longer a single guy and a single girl – they were a couple.

When Jimmy and Eugene finally came back to the table, they let Gladys and Edna pull them onto the dance floor. And though the two new wives greatly enjoyed the dance, they were perplexed by the brothers' fascination with the handsome older couple dancing near them.

Kate was in her own heaven sitting next to Ursula and Frankie, with her eyes on the dance floor. She and Ursula commented on their growing family, and how happy Eugene and Edna looked, and Jimmy and Gladys, and Jessica and Clem. And in silent wonder, they smiled at the new beginnings taking shape before their eyes – with Paul and Lucille, and Abe Creight and Anne Fletcher.

Frankie toddled over to Kate and she swept him up in her arms. "Do you see, Frankie? What life makes improbable, love makes probable."

Chapter 16

෧

Gabriel and Billy dashed to The Red String Curio Store after school, eager to see if the shop was busy. Business had increased over the past few days, with many customers commenting on the decorations and promising to return on the 14th. And now that Valentine's Day had arrived, Gabriel had his hopes up for a big success.

His face fell when he saw only a few people browsing, and only one customer at the counter. Henry and Junior were helping Dusty set out a large punch bowl with two dozen matching cups, all in pink-tinted glass.

Though Henry and Junior were dressed in their usual attire, Dusty had pulled out his professor's garb of a tweed jacket and a red bowtie.

Gabriel liked the cheerful touch. "You look nice, Dusty."

Dusty's hand went to the bowtie. "I thought it appropriate for the day."

"Come on, Billy. We need to get into our costumes and start drumming up business."

"Robin Hood to the rescue!"

"We'll go with you," said Junior. He tugged on Henry's arm and whispered. "Dusty may have beaten us in the last checkers round, but there's no need for him to outshine us now. Follow me."

They exchanged a few words with Mr. G, who was dressed in his scarlet embroidered waistcoat. He pointed them to the men's clothes and they were soon pulling out various items.

Junior found a bright red cummerbund and fastened it around his waist. "Just the thing!" Then he came upon a faded silk rose and tucked it into his lapel. He fished through the basket of ties and scarves, drew out a burgundy ascot, and handed it to Henry.

Henry held it up. "How does this thing work?"

"Loop it around your neck somehow."

Gabriel and Billy got into their host outfits and used the mirror in Mr. G's office to draw on mustaches, using the black wax pricing pencils. Gabriel fashioned himself a handlebar style along with a generous set of muttonchops, and Billy drew on a thin mustache and goatee. "Like Errol Flynn," he said, smiling at his reflection.

As Gabriel put on the finishing touches, he spotted the large poster for the window.

"Billy! The poster! We still have to finish it and put in the window."

"Let's do it now. I'll find something from my notes."

"Something simple, in big letters that people can't miss."

Billy flipped through the pages. "We already used most of these on the hearts. Here are Dusty's suggestions: 'Please, keep it to hearts and cupids.' 'Hearts galore.' Here we go!" Billy cried, holding up the notebook. "'Lonely Hearts!' It's short and catchy."

Gabriel tilted his head. "I thought he said 'Only Hearts.'"

Billy rechecked his notes. "I wrote down 'Lonely Hearts.' Besides, it sounds more familiar, doesn't it?"

"You're right. It does." They worked on filling in the large block letters. Billy was inspired to add a few jagged broken hearts, and he couldn't resist shooting an arrow into the largest of them with a few drops in red below it.

"Almost done."

Gabriel ran to the counter and grabbed the tape. "Hi, Mr. G. Everything looks in order. Billy and I will put up the poster and then we'll work on getting customers from the street."

Mr. G envisioned Billy grabbing old ladies and yanking them inside. "A gentle approach is always best. A welcoming hello. That sort of thing. I expect it will start to get busy, once the work-day ends."

The little bell rang and Tommy, Amy, and Mickey came in, carrying tins of cookies and treats.

"Greetings!" cried Mr. G. "Looks like the gang's all here."

Amy took off her coat and placed it in the small room behind the counter that served as office, kitchen, and general storeroom. She was dressed in a red dress and wore her long hair in a single braid down her back. She pushed up the sleeves to her dress, ready for action.

When she saw Gabriel and Billy, she broke into laughter. "Look at you two! Gabriel, I love your costume. And yours, Billy," she added with a touch of confusion. "Nice hats!"

"Billy and I are hosts."

"Hi, Mr. G," said Tommy. "Where should we put the stuff our moms made?"

"So much! We'll have the table filled with treats in no time. You can arrange everything next to the punch bowl. I've placed a few platters and a stack of small plates there. Dusty will assist you. He's preparing the punch."

"Mom will bring more when she and Dad come," said Amy, calling over her shoulder. "She decided to bake another batch of sugar cookies with pink icing."

Mr. G raised his eyebrows to Gabriel. "At least we'll be well fed." He let his eyes travel over his shop. "I'd say we're all set. Junior brought in a few more poems. We must have well over a dozen by now. I do hope we sell a few. He's put a lot of work into them."

After taping the poster to the window, Billy and Gabriel went back into the office. Billy slung the quiver over his shoulder and Gabriel grabbed the hand bell.

They gave a nod of approval to each other. "Let's go."

When they cut through the tables of merchandise, Gabriel suddenly stopped. "There's Mrs. Jenkins and her niece. Let's go say hi."

"Later," said Billy, pulling him along. "We need to get customers."

Little by little the shop began to fill. Mrs. Kuntzman arrived with Mrs. Wilson and her husband – all of them carrying platters and containers of cookies, ginger bread, and various Bavarian treats.

Outside the store, Gabriel rang the bell and Billy cried out, "Hear ye, hear ye! Happy hunting inside!"

Gabriel swept his arm to the store. "It's Valentine's Day – don't miss out on love! Your heart's desire awaits you inside!"

Billy added, "Books, birds, jewelry, and lots of red and pink stuff!"

When a few individual people stood before the poster and peered inside the window, Gabriel encouraged them to step into the store. "There's punch and treats and all kinds of interesting merchandise."

Billy was more direct and actually pushed them to the entrance. "Go inside where it's warm!" He opened the door and waved them in with big circular arm movements, as if he was herding cattle. "Inside! Come on – there you go!"

Every time a few people tentatively gathered in front of the poster, Billy ushered them into the store. Then he and Gabriel walked up and down the sidewalk and even across the street, ringing the bell and directing people to the party. From time to time, they stepped inside to warm up.

"Gabriel, Billy!" Mr. G waved them over to the counter. "Look who's here. Mrs. Jenkins and her niece."

The painfully shy girl with long braids pressed her lips together and kept her eyes on the floor.

"You remember Gabriel," said Mr. G, "and this is Billy."

"Hi, Bernice," said Gabriel.

"Bernice the niece!" cried Billy, which caused the girl to run away in tears.

Mrs. Jenkins threw her hands in the air. "There she goes again! Maybe you boys can cheer her up."

Billy turned to Gabriel and whispered. "Let's hide."

"We can't do that. We're the hosts!"

Mrs. Jenkins broke into a smile at seeing a group entering the shop. "Yoo-hoo!" She waved her fingers. "There's Harriet and the Hypatia Society."

Harriet came up to the counter, trailed by a dozen women. "Greetings, Mr. G. The shop looks positively splendid. We're delighted to be here. May I present Mrs. Cornelius Blevins, chairwoman of our club?"

"How do you do?" A prim, stout lady in a tweed suit presented herself and each member of her group. "Mind you, we're here in the spirit of celebration, whatever your sign might imply."

"Sign? Yes, well..." Mr. G showed as much interest as possible, while also answering questions from customers, and giving instructions to Gabriel and Billy about finding more cups for the punch. In between greeting the members, he leaned over to Tommy and Mickey. "Go find Dusty and Junior. Tell them I need assistance. Pronto!"

When Dusty and Junior were pulled away, Henry filled in at the punch bowl. Amy, who wanted to be at the front of the store to see everyone who came in, stepped in to help him.

Mr. G smiled as Dusty and Junior arrived at the counter. "Gentleman, may I present Mrs. Cornelius Blevins and the Hypatia Society. This is Augustus 'Junior' Evergreen – poet and calligrapher extraordinaire. And Professor Grover 'Dusty' Dillard – scholar, Egyptologist, and world traveler."

Dusty enjoyed the introduction and straightened his bow tie.

"Perhaps you two gentlemen can show the ladies around the shop and make sure they have some refreshment."

"It would be our pleasure," said Dusty, graciously bowing to the group.

Mr. G gave a sigh of relief and darted to the front of the store. He located Gabriel and Billy by the door chatting with Amy and sampling the cookies. "Go find Bernice. Get her involved somehow. I need to get back to the counter. I didn't expect quite so many people."

Billy rolled his eyes to the ceiling and headed to the back of the store with Gabriel.

"Ah, the renowned Hypatia," said Junior, also enjoying the attention of so many fair and learned women.

Dusty cut in, taking the lead. "Like your namesake, are you all mathematicians, scientists, and philosophers?" The skepticism in his tone was intended as good-natured.

But Mrs. Blevins bristled at the sarcasm and determined to set him straight. "We are all thinkers, Professor *Dusty*. Among us there are teachers, librarians, and writers. I myself taught mathematics for twenty years."

"Did you, indeed?" Dusty asked, not liking her tone.

"And she's a great traveler," said Harriet.

Mrs. Blevins scanned the vintage travel posters on the back wall and gazed at the Pyramids of Giza. "I have been to Egypt myself. Rode a camel to the Pyramids and the Sphinx. I even saw them at night, under a full moon. The most magical night of my life. Sailed down the Nile to the Valley of the Kings."

"Most impressive," said Dusty. Not to be outdone, he linked his hands behind him and wore his best professorial gaze – with a slight pinch to his eyebrows. "I have been thrice to Egypt, once to participate in an archeological dig. A most extraordinary experience." Not wanting to sound like a braggart, he added, with a self-deprecatory smile, "Alas, I have yet to see the Nubian pyramids." He gave a side glance to Mrs. Blevins. "Of the ancient Kushite kingdom, that is."

"I am well aware of the Kushite kingdom." Mrs. Blevins, finding herself upstaged by Dusty, couldn't resist a small jab. "I wonder you call yourself an Egyptologist, not having seen them."

Dusty colored in indignation. He was not accustomed to being challenged on his own turf. "I encountered unexpected problems concerning travel logistics. Such a seasoned adventurer as yourself must be acquainted with the difficulties of travel in a foreign land."

"I experienced no such problems," Mrs. Blevins replied airily, and raised her gaze to another poster. "Ah, the Levant. Land of the ancient Phoenicians. I've traveled there, as well. I recently gave a talk at our Society detailing my experience." She landed a superior smile on Dusty and Junior. "We host educational evenings once a month and often draw quite a crowd."

Her group of ladies nodded and smiled in pride.

Dusty grew more indignant as she continued to boast of all her travels. He couldn't wait to ditch the woman and her bevy of admirers.

They ended up at the punch bowl, which was now crowded. Unexpectedly so. When Dusty introduced the group to Henry and Amy, he once again attempted to reassert his status. "I made the punch myself, ladies. I do hope you enjoy it."

The ladies began to sip out of the delicate pink glass cups, nodding in appreciation. One of them complimented him and asked about the recipe.

Dusty gave a magnanimous smile. "Yes, it is delicious, isn't it? The famed recipe of my wife, Juniper."

Mrs. Blevins muttered, "Sounds like a shrub," and took a sip of the punch.

Dusty lost his composure and spoke louder than he intended. "A finer name than *Cornelius*!"

Harriet smiled sweetly. "Better known as Corny."

Junior hid his amusement by stuffing a cookie into his mouth.

"Corny! Now, there's a name," said Dusty, smiling widely at having stumbled upon metaphorical gold. He linked his hands behind his back and rocked on his heels. "Corny. Corny. Has a certain ring to it, doesn't it?"

Mrs. Blevins turned her back on the rude man and addressed Henry and Amy. They were soon discussing the merits of the Hypatia Society.

"It sounds so interesting," said Amy. "Can girls attend the lectures?"

"Why, of course." Once again, Mrs. Blevins was in her element, describing the monthly lectures to Amy, Henry, and Mrs. Kuntzman, who had just stopped by to refill her cup.

Dusty once more tried to eclipse the domineering woman by encouraging Henry to talk about his time riding with Teddy Roosevelt and the Rough Riders. Henry was soon entertaining the crowd around the punch bowl with tales of derring-do and youthful escapades.

Junior offered to take several members of the Hypatia club to his wall of framed poems.

Two of the women, best of friends, though they never agreed on anything, argued between themselves.

"A real poet! He looks just like Longfellow."

"I think he looks like Tennyson."

At the request of the more poetically-inclined members, Junior was soon reading the framed poems aloud to the ladies. Several of them decided to buy them on the spot.

Gabriel and Billy, meanwhile, had found Bernice by the rocking chairs, still sniffling.

"There you are!" cried Billy. "Why'd you run away?"

Her voice was barely audible. "You made fun of me. I hate my name."

"Bernice?" asked Billy. "What's wrong with that?"

"It's a nice name," added Gabriel.

With more volume she said, "I hate it. And I hate these braids. My aunt made me wear my hair like this. Like I'm eight years old. I'm twelve! And I hate this dress."

Billy threw open his hands to Gabriel in a "we tried" gesture.

"I have an idea!" said Gabriel. "How about you wear a costume, like us, and you can help us host."

"Me? A host?" She stood frozen in indecision, though a spark came to her eye.

"We could call you Bernie," offered Billy.

"That's a boy's name," she said, almost in tears again.

Billy tried variations, rubbing his chin in thought. "Bernella? Bernita? Bernessa?"

"You're smearing your beard. Are you making those up?"

"What's your middle name?" asked Gabriel.

"Rose," she said softly.

"How about we call you Bernice Rose?"

"Does that sound better?" asked Billy.

She nodded. She looked from Billy to Gabriel, barely able to ask the question that was filling her mind. "What kind of costume?"

"Let's go take a look. Follow us!" said Gabriel.

They ran to the counter and told Mr. G about their plan.

"A splendid idea. There's a lovely floral shawl on the mannequin in back. And perhaps a hat!" he called out after them.

They were already running down the aisle to the clothing area. Bernice loved the shawl and tied it different ways, settling on draping it over one shoulder and tying it at her waist. "It hides most of my dress," she said in triumph.

Billy offered a red velvet hat. "And this will hide your hair."

"Thanks, Billy," she said, tucking her braids inside.

"Much better." Billy gave a firm nod.

She looked in the mirror and smiled. "I don't even look like me!"

"Let's go show Mr. G and ask him where he needs us," said Gabriel.

Several people stood at the counter waiting to purchase items.

Mr. G appeared elated by the crowd. "Thank goodness, you're here. Go find a few more folding chairs and scatter them about. This is turning into a Valentine's Day extravaganza! It's like Christmas. I didn't expect it."

Amy's parents arrived carrying several tins of treats. "Hello, Mr. G!" said Mrs. Little. "I don't believe you've met my husband. Amy has told us all about the Valentine's Day party and we are thrilled to be here. Thrilled!" She leaned into Mr. G. "How clever of you to tie in Valentine's Day with the love-lorn." In response to Mr. G's raised eyebrows, she added with a wink: "The poster in the window."

"The poster? I can't take credit for the art-work. The children made all the signs and a fine job they did."

She gave a hoot of a laugh and squeezed her husband's arm. "The children! Oh, he's such a tease, isn't he? Now, where shall we bring the cookies?"

Mickey and Tommy had been helping at the counter, and when Mr. G gave a small nod to them, they offered to show Mrs. and Mr. Little to the table up front.

Gabriel slipped behind the counter and showed Bernice and Billy how to wrap the items in brown paper and tie the package with red string. When there was a momentary lull, Mr. G praised Bernice.

"That's quite a transformation, Bernice."

"She's Bernice Rose now," Billy explained.

"And seeing that it's Valentine's Day..." Mr. G sorted through the necklaces hanging on a display at the counter. He lifted a long strand of pink glass beads and handed it to her. "For your costume."

Her eyes lit up at the long flapper-style neck-lace. "Thank you, Mr. G. They're beautiful!" She looped them over her hat and smiled.

Mr. G looked up and saw a bottleneck at the door. "Perhaps one of you could show the customers inside, bring them to the refreshments. They're standing outside, as if they're afraid to come in."

"I'll take care of that," cried Billy, and ran to the front and out the door, followed by Bernice Rose.

Mrs. Blevins and several members of the club made themselves comfortable around the checkers table, along with a few other people. She was regaling them with tales of her trip to Istanbul when a half dozen of her acolytes ran up to her.

"Gerty! This is it!"

Mrs. Gertrude Blevins raised her chin. "Could you be more specific, Velma?"

"The special occasion! This is the special occasion we've been waiting for!"

The two friends, for once, agreed. "Our dandelion wine!"

"Gerty" turned to Junior to explain. "One of our members has a home upstate and instructed us on the making of dandelion wine."

"Can we?"

"I don't see why not. Constance, you have the key to the storeroom. It's only a few blocks away." She scooted them away with her fingers. "Well, hurry along then. I fancy a glass myself."

The little bell on the door rang and rang, and the cash register clanged and clanged, and the shop continued to fill up. Several shy men and women parked themselves near the cookie and punch table so that they would have something to do, something to fill their hands with, as they glanced around.

Mr. G studied the crowd with a puzzled expression. As Billy and Bernice dashed by, he stopped them.

"Billy, I want you to try an experiment for me. Perhaps you could casually introduce a few people. The ones who are keeping to themselves —"

Before he could explain in more detail, Billy and Bernice Rose ran to the front and started talking to people, asking their names and introducing them to each other.

Mr. G kept glancing to the entrance as he rang up sales. "I just don't understand it. Quite the mystery. Why, they're pouring in!"

Gabriel, who had been helping Tommy and Amy at the punch bowl, now ran back to the counter, followed by Billy and Bernice Rose. "Dusty said the punch bowl is getting low. What should we do?"

Gertrude Blevins, seated in the leather wing-back chair, overheard the concern. "Never fear, Mr. G! We'll soon fill the punch bowl with our summer project."

Her audience had grown and she was now describing their summer excursion for dandelions. She was a born raconteur. Even Dusty, against his will, found himself fascinated by her stories, and parked himself near the checkers circle.

Mr. G leaned over to Gabriel, Billy, and Bernice Rose. "In the meantime, go to the kitchen cupboard and round up more drinks. I purchased colas and root beers in the off chance that we would need them. Bring them — and — anything else you can find. And pour the drinks yourself to make them last longer." Again, Billy ran off, followed closely by Bernice Rose.

"And Gabriel," he called after him, "search the place for more glasses and cups."

"I know just the thing," said Gabriel. "The Toby mugs!"

After they located the trove of drinks in the office, the trio rounded up as many drinking vessels as they could find and set them near the punch bowl, on the checkers table, and on top of the glass counters where several young men and women demurely stood.

Then they made trip after trip with soda bottles and filled up cups and mugs and glasses. Bernice Rose, delighting in her new role, never stopped smiling. While rummaging around the office, Billy came across several bottles of a tawny-colored liquid, which he also poured into the awaiting glasses, making introductions while he was at it.

Soon the Hypatia club members had the punch bowl filled again, this time with honey-colored wine. The noise level increased as the customers ate and drank and chatted and shopped and laughed.

Mr. G sold the framed poems, and red and pink merchandise, cupids and anything with hearts, and even a birdcage with two porcelain crows inside. He racked his brain trying to think how he could get the crowd to spread out. They were congregating just inside the door and hugging the refreshment table. And curiously, they gathered outside in the cold, in front of the poster. He was actually glad for Billy's insistence that they come inside.

"Gabriel!" he cried. "Can you man the counter? I have an idea on how to get people to move to the middle of the store. The piano!"

Mr. G went to the old upright, opened the lid, and began playing and singing "Beautiful Dreamer."

That was all it took. A crowd soon gathered around him, many of them singing along. Billy and Bernice Rose continued to fill glasses, while Tommy and Mickey helped Amy and Henry by washing plates and cups in the tiny office kitchen and returning them to the table.

Mrs. Little heard the piano and hurried over with her second cup of dandelion wine. She planted herself next to Mr. G as he sorted through some sheet music.

"I'm in my element now!" she said. "I'll take over here, Mr. G – you have customers to tend to." And with a side thrust of her rather ample hips, she scooted him off the bench.

"Oh, Mr. Little!" she called out. "My official page turner," she explained to the growing crowd. Mr. Little, holding a Toby mug depicting a seafaring scallywag, turned the pages as his wife sang. Her voice was soon filling all the corners and nooks of the store, and even spilled out onto the sidewalk when the door opened and closed.

Mr. G returned to the counter, relieved to have dispersed people throughout the store. The register continued to ring all evening. "This is unheard of Gabriel. A resounding success!"

"Billy and Bernice Rose are asking everybody their names and introducing them to each other. That seems to help."

"I've noticed that," said Mr. G, rubbing his chin. "It's almost as if people are pairing up."

"It *is* Valentine's Day."

"Yes, it is. And the first one after the war. Still…"

They rang up yet another framed poem and looked across to where Junior had a circle of women around him as he delivered lines from well-known poems. Several women sighed at the romantic figure he cut, the melodic words pouring forth from his poet's heart.

The two friends from the Hypatia Society, with glasses of the special occasion drink in their hands, challenged Junior to a sort of match. Junior entertained them by switching back and forth between Longfellow and Tennyson, American accent and British accent.

"Tennyson!" cried one of them.

Junior pulled on his beard and recited: *"A man had given all other bliss, And all his worldly worth for this, To waste his whole heart in one kiss, Upon her perfect lips."*

"Now Longfellow!" cried the other friend.

Junior's arm reached out. *"Tell me not, in mournful numbers, Life is but an empty dream! For the soul is dead that slumbers, And things are not what they seem. Life is real! Life is earnest! And the grave is not its goal —"*

"More Tennyson!"

Junior took a moment, and then spoke solemnly. *"I hold it true, whate'er befall; I feel it when I sorrow most; 'Tis better to have loved and lost, Than never to have loved at all."*

"Longfellow!"

"Between the dark and the daylight, When the night is beginning to lower..."

The two friends called out the switch until the lines grew shorter and shorter, faster and faster.

"Tennyson!"

Junior spread open his arms. *"Who are wise in love, Love most, say least."*

"Longfellow!"

In a lively staccato he recited: *"By the shore of Gitche Gumme, by the shining Big-Sea-Water..."*

"Tennyson!"

Junior playfully held up his arms, warding off the onslaught of poetic demands: *"Cannon to right of them, Cannon to left of them..."*

A chorus of laughter and applause followed, along with requests for more framed poems in his beautiful calligraphy.

Dusty sat at the checkers tables with Mrs. Blevins, both of them now mellowed by the fragrant summer quaff. They had each profusely apologized to the other on discovering that their spouses were long since deceased, and agreed that both "Juniper" and "Cornelius" were highly dignified names. And holding small etched glasses of golden sweetness, they reminisced about the romance of travel and past enchantments.

With an indulgent sigh, Dusty asked, "And did you really see the Pyramids under a full moon?"

*

Charles arrived home and was greeted by Lillian wearing a crimson velvet dress and her crystal brooch. Her eyes filled with pleasure at the bunch of red, white, and pink roses in his arms.

"Oh, Charles! They're beautiful."

"I know we have to hurry to the Red String, but I have a surprise for you first."

As Lillian filled a vase with water and placed the roses inside, she called over her shoulder. "And I have a surprise for you!"

She stopped what she was doing and ran to Charles. "Oh, guess what?" and tears darted to her smiling eyes.

He looped his arms around her. "What? What is it?"

Lillian could barely get the words out. "I had a telegram."

"Izzy?" he asked.

"They're getting married. Today! On Valentine's Day."

"That means they're already married," he said, squeezing her.

"It finally happened! I'm so happy. I can't wait for them to come back."

They bundled up Charlotte and brought the carriage downstairs. Lillian could barely contain her happiness. "This is turning out to be the best Valentine's Day ever."

"And it's not over yet," added Charles.

They began to walk briskly towards The Red String Curio Store. But then Charles took a turn in the opposite direction.

Lillian looked up at him in surprise.

"This will just take a minute."

They walked to a large apartment building a block from Central Park and were greeted by a real estate agent standing outside.

"Charles?" Lillian asked, as they were shown inside.

"I wanted to give you more choices," he said with a smile.

Lillian caught her breath. "You mean…?"

"We don't have to leave the neighborhood to have more room, do we?"

They stepped inside a paneled elevator and got off on the fifth floor. The agent opened a door and stepped inside a beautiful entryway. He showed them around the spacious apartment, pointing out the parquet floors, the trimmed high ceilings, and the carved mantel over the fireplace.

Charles excitedly showed her the three bedrooms and a large alcove that could serve as a studio.

Lillian exclaimed at each detail, scarcely believing what she was seeing. In the alcove she stood in the middle and turned around, imagining a table, shelves of supplies, and light pouring through the windows.

Charles saw the delight in her eyes and filled with happiness. "The kitchen's not much larger than the one we have now, but the appliances are newer and bigger."

Lillian ran her hand over the counter, the refrigerator. "I love it! And it's much bigger."

Lillian was torn between laughing and crying. She walked from room to room exclaiming, "It's perfect! It's absolutely perfect. The boys will be so happy."

Reluctantly, she left with Charles. They arranged to see the apartment again in the daytime over the weekend when they could bring the boys.

Back outside, Lillian stepped back to gaze up at the beautiful building. "I don't think I could be any happier. Can we really live there?"

Charles was holding Charlotte and rocked her back and forth. "We can move next month, if you like."

She reached up to kiss him, and then wiggled Charlotte's hands. "We're going to love it, here, aren't we, Charlotte?"

After another kiss, they made their way to the Red String, Lillian almost floating in happiness.

They stopped in amazement at the crowd. The shop was packed, with music and singing pouring out the door. Couples were leaving arm in arm, many of them with packages wrapped in paper and tied with red string, and others were still arriving.

They stepped inside and were soon greeted by Henry and Mrs. Kuntzman at the punch bowl. Henry poured them two glasses of dandelion wine, while Mrs. Kuntzman cooed over Charlotte.

The raffle was just beginning, and Mr. G let Amy and Bernice Rose draw and read out the winning names. Three of Junior's poems were given as prizes, followed by a flurry of cheers and clapping and congratulations, and Mr. G taking orders for more.

"Dad!" Tommy ran up to Charles and Lillian.

"Hello, Tom," Charles said, draping his arm around Tommy's shoulder. "This is quite an event!"

"It's better than we expected," he said excitedly. "Mom, look who's here!"

Lillian turned around to see Matty Cavendish – standing! With a cane, but still, it was the first time she had seen him without a wheelchair.

"Matty!" She looked him up and down.

"Hello, Mrs. Drooms. I've made some progress since the last time you saw me. Have you met my fiancée? Carol, these are Tommy and Gabriel's parents."

"So pleased to meet you!" Carol said excitedly. "Gabriel talked us into coming and we're ever so glad we did. Look!" She held up a framed poem. "I was one of the winners!"

Matty took Carol's arm. "We're going to try to find a place for dinner."

"Good night," said Carol. "And Happy Valentine's Day!"

"Happy Valentine's Day!" Lillian called back to them. She squeezed Tommy's shoulder. "I'm so proud of you two. And look at this crowd!"

Lillian scanned the store, searching for Gabriel. There he was, talking to two elderly women, apparently enjoying the conversation as much as they were. Just then Gabriel looked up and waved at her. He said something to the two women, who smiled at Lillian, and then snaked his way through the crowd.

"You're here!" cried Gabriel. They all talked over one another about the success of the party, meeting Matty and his fiancée, and pointing out all the neighbors who were there. Gabriel leaned down to Charlotte and kissed her cheek. "Happy Valentine's Day, Charlotte! Your first one."

Tommy and Amy took over at the punch bowl so that Henry and Mrs. Kuntzman could sit down and visit with everyone.

Gabriel showed Lillian and Charles the tables of merchandise, and brought them to the counter to talk with Mr. G. Then he introduced them to members of the Hypatia Society, Mrs. Jenkins and Bernice Rose, and some of his new acquaintances.

After visiting with their friends and neighbors, and listening to Mrs. Little sing a few songs, Lillian and Charles found seats near the checkers table next to Henry and Mrs. Kuntzman. Mrs. Blevins and other members were making plans for future lectures.

"Perhaps you, Dusty, would like to be a guest lecturer one month and discuss your travels?"

He gave a deep nod. "It would be my pleasure."

The two friends, seated on either side of Junior, added, "And Junior could come and talk about poetry!"

Mrs. Blevins turned to Henry. "And Mr. Hankel, you must come and discuss your time as a Rough Rider."

"That'd be just dandy," said Henry, pulling off the uncomfortable neck cloth and setting it aside.

Harriet placed her hand on Mrs. Kuntzman's arm. "And perhaps we could persuade our new friend Martha to do a cooking demonstration."

"Ladies," said Gertrude Blevins, "I do believe we've found a treasure trove of talent here at The Red String Curio Store. Let's raise our glasses to Mr. G!"

An odd assortment of glasses and teacups and Toby mugs were lifted in his name. He gave a small nod of appreciation as he rang up another customer.

Gabriel and Billy were back at the counter, helping Mr. G wrap up purchases and tie them in red string.

Bernice had made friends with Amy and was helping her and Tommy with the refreshments. They soon came up to Mr. G to announce that the punch bowl was empty and only a few cookies were left.

Mr. G looked out fondly over his store. "And the crowd is thinning out. Alas, I think our Valentine's Day party is coming to a close. My heartiest of thanks to you all."

"Shall we start cleaning up?" asked Amy.

"No, no. It's Valentine's Day!" Mr. G said with a laugh. "Time to be off with your families."

"We'll come back tomorrow, Mr. G," said Tommy.

"And help put everything back in order," added Mickey.

"Only if you agree to a little remuneration for all your hard work," said Mr. G.

"You mean money?" Billy asked with a wide smile.

"I certainly do," Mr. G answered, laughing. "I couldn't have done it without you. Or my trusty assistant." He tapped Gabriel on his bowler and addressed him. "Our shelves are quite depleted. What say you we go on our first scouting expedition for the rare and unusual?"

Gabriel nodded. "Modern day rag n' bone men!"

"Can I come?" asked Billy.

"We'd be honored," replied Mr. G.

The crowd began to disperse, though by the sound of it, many of the couples were moving on to dinner or clubs to continue the Valentine's Day celebration.

Lillian leaned closer to Charles. "It's strange, but I have the impression that a lot of these couples just met."

"I was thinking the same thing. Especially some of the younger people." He shook his head in puzzlement. "Let's go find a few items to buy. See what's left."

Lillian chose a book of poetry with a red cover and a set of ruby glass candleholders – "for our new home!" And at Gabriel's urging, they bought the jolly Toby mug innkeeper.

Tommy wanted to purchase a red heart brooch for Amy, but Mr. G wouldn't let him pay for it. Amy was delighted and said she was going to wear it every Valentine's Day for the rest of her life.

And when Billy asked how much the green hat with the feather cost, Mr. G said he could keep it.

"We'll all meet here tomorrow after school," said Amy. "I'll wash the dishes so they don't get broken."

"And I'll gather up the hearts," said Billy. "We'll save them for next year."

Lillian and Charles saw the sadness that crossed Gabriel and Tommy's faces believing that they would not be there next year.

"Let's go to the diner," said Charles. "We have some news we want to share with you boys."

Tommy walked Amy to the front door as she left with her parents, and Gabriel and Billy folded their waistcoats at the front counter.

The Hypatia club left, saying their goodbyes, and the shop slowly emptied. Junior dozed in his armchair, and next to him Dusty sat gazing up at the travel posters of Egypt, empty glass in hand. Henry and Mrs. Kuntzman, arms linked, headed home to the rouladen and potato dumplings that awaited them.

Harriet, Mr. and Mrs. Jenkins, and Bernice Rose came to the counter to say goodbye to everyone. Bernice had returned the shawl and hat and now handed the strand of pink beads to Mr. G.

"Thank you for letting me help out and for wearing this beautiful necklace. I felt so grown up all night and I wasn't shy at all!"

Mr. G took the necklace and draped it over her head. "You can keep it. I'd say you earned it."

"I can? Truly?" She gave him a hug. "Thank you, Mr. G!" She turned to Gabriel and Billy.

"Thanks for letting me be a host with you. That was the most fun I ever had!" She turned around at the door and hollered back to them, "I'll see you next time I come to visit."

Billy gave a big wave. "We'll be waiting for you, Bernice Rose! We'll think of another event to host. So long!"

Gabriel raised his eyebrows at Billy.

Billy shrugged. "She's a fun girl. Once she stopped being the old Bernice."

Gabriel took a closer look and Billy and began to laugh. He had rubbed at his face all night, smudging his goatee and mustache so that now his face simply looked dirty.

Lillian put Charlotte in the carriage, amazed that she wasn't bothered by all the commotion. They slowly took their leave, saying goodnight to Mr. G and a few neighbors who lingered, reluctant to leave the gaiety.

Tommy and Gabriel led the way to the diner, talking about the evening and how Billy must have pulled fifty people into the store from the sidewalk.

They walked in the opposite direction of the one they arrived, so that Lillian only now saw the large poster in the window with the border she had painted. She took in a sharp breath and stood rooted to the sidewalk and as she read the words in bold letters:

LONELY HEARTS

with a picture of a dripping, broken heart below it.

"Charles!" she cried, covering her smile with both hands. She grabbed his arm as he came back with the carriage. "Charles, look!"

He had the same moment of surprise. "Well, that explains it!" he said, and they burst into laughter. They stood a moment before the Valentine's Day poster and leaned into each other.

Lillian raised her face to Charles and kissed his cheek. "They'll have to keep it for next year's party."

"Indeed, they will," he laughed.

And they hurried to catch up with Tommy and Gabriel.

Made in the USA
Las Vegas, NV
10 February 2023